Total-E-Bound Publishing books by Justine Elyot:

Competitive Nature
Sempre
Honeytrapped
The Sevarian Way
A Very Personal Trainer
Bollywood Superstar
The Science of Submission

Food of Love

HIGHLY STRUNG

JUSTINE ELYOT

HIGHLY STRUNG

Dedication

To all the musicians, especially the viola player from the BSO I had a crush on when I was 14.

Chapter One

Of all the days for a bomb scare on the Victoria Line, they had to choose this one.

Lydia Foster hugged her new violin case, stripped now of all the shiny stickers and stars of her battered but beloved student number, as the strip lights flickered on and off. Despite the ominous situation, most of the occupants continued reading their newspapers and listening to their iPods, well used to sudden and inexplicable standstills in dark tunnels. But Lydia could not be so sanguine. She checked her watch, agitated, and puffed out her cheeks when the long and short hands gave her news she didn't want.

"Are you late for a concert?"

She almost jumped out of her seat. People just didn't talk to you on Tube trains, but the white-haired gentleman to her left didn't seem to know this rule.

"Um, no. A rehearsal, actually," she said, when she'd made all the usual lightspeed calculations — *Is he a maniac? Will he ask me weird, pervy questions? Would it be very rude of me to ignore him?*

"I always wanted to play the violin," the man confided. "Are you in a string quartet?"

"No, an orchestra. It's my first day. First rehearsal. So I really don't want to be late." She sighed, looking up and down the carriage as if this might set the train back in motion.

"An orchestra! Professional?"

"Yes. The Westminster Symphony."

The man took a breath and nodded, gratifyingly awed. Lydia loved the reception she got when she told people she was with the WSO. *I have arrived.*

"You'll be working with that Milan fellow." The gentleman chuckled. "Quite a character. Did you watch *The Next Big String*?"

Lydia blushed. Of course she had. Her massive crush on first violinist Milan Kaspar had been a large part of her reason for auditioning for the orchestra in the first place.

"Of course, they always have to have the Big Bad Judge on those talent contests," mused Lydia's companion. "I'm sure he's nothing like that in real life. Rather difficult to work with otherwise, I should imagine. Oh, but I shouldn't be saying this to you on your first day. I'm sure your nerves are bad enough as it is."

Lydia coughed out a half-laugh. "Uh huh," she managed to say. Her face felt as if it were on fire. All she could think about was the crafty morning orgasm she had teased out of her tense body, thinking about Milan Kaspar judging her playing, finding it wanting and giving her a little private lesson of his own. But why would he be interested in her, when rumour had it he had been seeing Tilda Fox-Boyce, the patrician and perfectly-coiffed presenter of the television programme? Of course he wouldn't.

"Good-looking chap, though. I'm sure he has his pick of the ladies."

Before Lydia could reply to this inflammatory remark, the train juddered into life.

"Due to a bomb scare at Victoria, all passengers are advised to alight at Pimlico. I repeat…" The intercom droned on.

"Fuck," Lydia swore under her breath. She would have to walk the last part of the journey, since Pimlico Station didn't link up to any other Tube line.

"Good luck."

"Thanks. I'll need it."

As the curving, white-tiled station wall slid past the windows, she readied her violin case, preparing for a shuffle, then a sprint.

Out in the sludgy, grey cold of a January afternoon in London, Lydia raced up Vauxhall Bridge Road. Her heart pounded and her legs turned to mush, but she didn't stop until she arrived at the building, just off the end of the road, which acted as the orchestra's rehearsal space.

Reaching the door, she gasped for breath, doubling over her violin case. She was half an hour late.

"Fucksticks," she panted, entering the empty lobby and following the muffled musical sounds coming from a set of doors halfway down a staircase.

Nobody noticed her when she pushed one door open and sidled in as unobtrusively as she could, hiding in an obscure corner until an obvious moment to introduce herself arrived.

She took the opportunity to watch the orchestra, her eyes settling quickly and naturally on the person she most wanted to check out—Milan Kaspar.

Oh, my God—there he was, in the flesh. She could only see his back and part of the side of his head, his violin wedged between firm chin and broad shoulder, his caramel-coloured hair flying as he bowed. He always gave the music his all, thought Lydia, starry-eyed, her pulse jumping high. It was as if he and his instrument were one. What were they playing? Something Viennese and waltzy, by the sounds of it. Oh, yes—Weber's *Invitation to the Dance*.

The music made Lydia feel joyous and light-spirited. Despite the long run up Vauxhall Bridge Road, she felt an urge to twirl around and dance. If only she were wearing a flouncy taffeta skirt instead of jeans and Converse trainers. She bounced discreetly on the soles of her feet, swaying to the infectious beat, moving forward into the room until the woman at the back on percussion caught sight of her, turned and smiled a welcome.

The music stopped abruptly and Josh Clayton shook his head and folded his arms. Lydia recognised him as the conductor who had auditioned her, along with two of the trustees and a random violinist—Milan had been away filming.

"No, no, no, this is dragging. Some of you aren't following my beat."

"Some of us aren't *seeing* your beat."

The deep, accented voice was unmistakable. Lydia almost dissolved in a pool of lust on hearing Milan's famously dark tones.

"Yes, well, we've had this discussion before," said Clayton irritably. "And it always ends up the same way. Keep your eye on the baton and you won't miss a thing."

"But we do!" a violinist to Milan's right objected. "I didn't catch the change in tempo at *vivace* at all."

"What do you want? A signpost?"

Lydia grimaced at Clayton's obvious exasperation.

"It might help," said Milan dryly.

"Listen, I can't make this any more obvious! I've never worked with such a bunch of mules in my life. What is wrong with you people?"

"Mules!" A cellist stood up, shoulders back, spoiling for a fight. Despite the aggressive stance, Lydia thought he must have been one of the most beautiful men she had ever seen, if you liked pale, delicate youths with eyelashes like road sweepers. On balance, she preferred the more muscular Milan, but all the same, she found herself mesmerised by the cellist's bottomless eyes. "Do not insult us! We are musicians, not animals!"

"If you're musicians, prove it!" thundered Clayton. Then, clutching his forehead, "Oh, you know what? Forget it. I'm done here. Fuck you. Good luck."

He flung his baton to the ground and marched off, pushing Lydia out of his way with his shoulder so that she fell gracelessly to the floor in his wake.

"Oh my God, are you okay?" The female percussionist rushed over and knelt by her side, transmitting a strong waft of Armani Diamonds to Lydia's nostrils.

"Yes, yes, fine, just a bump." Lydia allowed the woman to help her up.

When she looked over towards Milan, she noticed him high-fiving the cellist, while a great deal of rowdy laughter and gossip seemed to be going on.

"Are you the new violinist? Sorry you've seen us like this, what an introduction." The woman patted Lydia down, tutting. She was very Mother Hen-ish for such a sleek and glamorous-looking woman, Lydia thought. There wasn't a hair of her black bob out of place, and her makeup looked professionally applied.

"I'm Vanessa, on percussion, as I'm sure you've worked out. Welcome to the WSO. Oh, dear. Milan's so naughty."

Vanessa shook her head as they both watched the first violinist hold court in the centre of the string section before mounting the conductor's podium, taking his place as the orchestra's leader.

He held his bow in the air and waved it with one powerful arm. Silence fell.

"Okay!" he said, eyes flashing, a picture of triumph and exuberance. "We are, once more, minus a conductor. But we still work! The music can still be played. For now, I lead from the violin. Yes?"

Some applause and a few ragged cheers indicated approval of Milan's words.

"You are learning," he said with a wicked flash of a grin. "In my country, we are experienced in revolution. More than you British. But you are learning."

God, he was even more handsome in the flesh, if that was remotely possible. Lydia drank in his strong, rangy body, his arrogant posture, his high cheekbones and prominent nose. The gesture he had performed so often on *The Next Big String* — the sweep of the brow and toss of the hair — was such a familiar lust-trigger that Lydia's knees weakened. He was six feet and one inch of undiluted charisma and he was…oh, God. He was looking straight at her.

He jabbed his bow in her direction.

"Who are you?"

Dozens of necks swivelled, dozens of pairs of eyes roved over Lydia, who shrank back self-consciously.

"Er, Lydia Foster. Violinist."

He frowned and she quailed.

"You are late."

"Sorry. Bomb scare on the Victoria Line." The words came out somehow, but they sounded foreign. And what was this meek, squeaky little voice?

"Bombs? We let bombs stand between us and our music? No. We don't."

Lydia tried to breathe in, but found that her lungs were full. Her urge to scream '*Stop staring!*' at the rest of the orchestra was mercifully quashed by the closed-up state of her throat.

Milan waved his bow impatiently.

"Come on, then," he snapped. "Sit down. Get your violin out."

Eyes fixed on the floor, Lydia scurried through the banks of chairs to the back row of the first violins, too mortified to hear Milan's subsequent words about how to play the Weber piece to his satisfaction. Her fingers fumbled with the catch of her case and she almost broke a string trying to get the instrument out, conscious of the curious gazes of all the other violinists.

"Nice fiddle," whispered the middle-aged man next to her, a note of sympathy in his voice. "Don't worry about Milan. That's just the way he is. It isn't personal."

"No?" she whispered back, grateful for the reassurance.

"He'll have forgotten all about it by the time we've finished this piece." The man winked, settling his chin on the edge of his instrument, bow poised across the strings.

Lydia thought she ought to do the same. Milan finished his spiel and came off the platform to his chair on the outer perimeter of the first violinists, though he remained standing, needing to be visible to the whole orchestra.

He held up his bow for a few seconds before counting in the beautiful cellist, who played the opening bars solo before being joined by the woodwind for the slow introduction.

Lydia watched the cellist's smooth, dark hair fall, fringing his face as he bent over his instrument. Then Milan raised his bow, ready for the tumble into waltz tempo, and she began to play.

Surrounded by exhilarating dance music, Lydia forgot the woes of the moment and became nothing but a bow hand and fingers pressing on strings, her head whirling along with the imaginary waltzers, keeping pace with the black notes that whizzed past her eyes. Yes, she belonged here. Yes, this was right. Everything would be all right after all.

Incredible to think that she was working with the man whose deft bowing she followed, taking her cue from the speed of his arm and the wild flying of his hair. *I am working with Milan Kaspar! I am his colleague!*

It was two hours before they made it to the end of the piece, two hours of stopping and starting, picking every phrase apart, being shouted at or coaxed or charmed by Milan along the way. Once those two hours were over, Lydia felt that she had fought and won a battle. She was a member of the orchestra now and it held her undying loyalty.

"Good, that's good, that's promising." Milan, clearly enjoying his new conducting role, treated the orchestra to a full-beam smile. "We see what tomorrow brings when Clayton hands in his resignation. I hope the Trust will think we can do this."

'I *can do this*', *you mean*, thought Lydia cynically, packing away her violin.

She was craning her neck, looking for the friendly percussionist, planning to invite her for a post-rehearsal coffee, when her attention was distracted by an imperious click of the fingers.

"You. New girl."

Lydia couldn't quite believe it, but Milan was pointing at her, his eyes intent. He tossed his head and beckoned a long, pale finger.

Struggling to contain her breath, Lydia trotted up to him, wondering whether to expect an apology, a welcome, a scolding or a proposition, or something else completely.

"You know where Chappell's is?" he asked brusquely.

"Of course." Everyone knew where Chappell's was. It was the most famous music shop in the UK.

He fumbled in his pocket and proffered a twenty-pound note.

"I need an A string. Eudoxa."

Lydia's mouth fell open. She looked from Milan to the banknote and back again. He was serious.

"Well? Why wait? Take it. I'll be in the Delius Arms. You know it?"

"Next door," said Lydia, taking the note before she could stop herself.

"Good, good. I'll see you there."

He nodded formally then swung around, dismissing her in favour of a group of other string players who appeared to be waiting for him.

Chapter Two

Lydia crumpled the twenty pounds in her fist, dumbfounded by irritation.

Armani Diamonds signalled an advance warning of Vanessa the percussionist's presence. "What's he done?"

"He...he expects me to run his errands for him!"

"Oh dear. He's a terrible prima donna, you know. Well, you saw him on TV, I expect."

"Why the hell did I say yes? Why did I take this money?"

"Believe me, it's easier than saying no. I'm not sure anyone's ever said no to Milan."

"He's like a hypnotist," agreed Lydia. "But a spectacularly twatty and annoying one."

"Ah well. What's he asked you to do?"

"Get him a new string from Chappell's. But it's in Soho! Bloody miles away."

"I'll come with you if you like."

"Oh, would you? Thanks. We can get a coffee or something after."

"I'd love to. Come on then, before it gets too dark out there. I hate the winter, don't you?"

"Mmm."

Bitter rain was falling in the street outside and the light was dull enough to justify headlights on the buses and taxis thundering past.

Lydia had exaggerated the distance from Victoria to Soho — in better weather, it would be a pleasant walk around the perimeter of Buckingham Palace, over Green Park and along Piccadilly, but today the prospect was far from appealing. She and Vanessa headed down below ground, assuming from the lack of warning chalkboards and yellow cones that the bomb scare was over.

"So what was going on today?" asked Lydia as their train jolted out of the station. "With Clayton? Why were the violinists playing at the wrong tempo? I didn't think his conducting was *that* bad."

"It wasn't. He's a good conductor." Vanessa sighed. "It's Milan. He's got it into his head that, if he scares off enough conductors, the Trust will offer him the gig."

"What?" Lydia stared. "Do the trustees know about this?"

"No, no. Well, not explicitly. Milan's pretty good at not getting caught out, and he's got at least two-thirds of the orchestra on side. The others just don't want to get involved."

"Surely they'll start to suspect, if enough conductors walk out."

"They won't want to lose Milan. He's a celeb now. Audiences have been stratospheric since that silly talent show. They all want to see the man in action."

Can't say I blame them. Shame he's such a knob, though. Such a gorgeous, sexy...ugh.

"He is rather...you know." Lydia bit her lip, giving Vanessa a sidelong glance.

"Oh, no, my girl, don't go there," said Vanessa firmly. "We've lost too many good players that way. He's a heartbreaker. He's too wrapped up in himself to offer anything useful to anyone else. Steer clear."

"I had a feeling you'd say that." Lydia sighed.

"He never wanted to be an orchestral player, not that he's ever said so," continued Vanessa. "But he can't be part of a team. He has to be the leader, the one that stands out, the one in control. I think he wanted a virtuoso career, but it didn't work out and now everyone's paying for it."

"He *could* have been a virtuoso, though. He's a fantastic violinist. And with the charisma of Paganini too."

"Hush, don't let him hear you say that! He's unbearable enough as it is."

"It's such a shame."

"Don't," barked Vanessa, "go there."

"I get the message! I won't go there! But isn't he seeing that Tilda from the telly?"

"I think they split," said Vanessa vaguely. "We get off here, don't we?"

"Oh, yeah. Dangerous game, though, isn't it? Trying to get the conductors to quit. What if the orchestra's reputation goes down the pan?"

"It won't. He's clever enough to be all sweetness and light every time we do a recital with a guest conductor. We've had stellar endorsements from the likes of Simon Rattle and Valery Gergiev. He just gaslights the salaried ones until they throw in the towel. Or the baton."

"Wow, quite sneaky."

"Yes. Not a nice man, Lydia."

"No. Right."

A sleety dusk was falling in Wardour Street, and they were Chappell's last customers before closing time, hastily slapping down the twenty pounds, taking their change and heading back out into the gathering gloom.

"He said he'd be in the Delius Arms. God, I don't know if I can face rush hour on the Tube again. Shall we walk back?"

"Oh, go on. I've got my umbrella."

Vanessa sheltered them both as they made their way through the city, weaving in and out of all the people on their way home from work. Lydia often thought that her special superpower should be feet that could walk endless distances — she loved to tramp the streets of London and found it frustrating that she could only manage a few miles at a time. Even in the cold and dark, she found enchantment in its vastness and its endless possibilities.

Lifting her face to the icy drops, shivering but not miserable, she reminded herself again that she was a violinist with the Westminster Symphony Orchestra. No matter what life threw at her by way of imperious men and shambolic relationships with conductors, nobody was going to take that away from her.

The Delius Arms was warm and cheery, but Lydia felt the need to dive into the ladies' toilets to check herself in the mirror before completing her errand. Her hair was stuffed inside the hood of her parka and her face was red with cold and streaked with rain, her spectacles steaming up rapidly in the more temperate air. Nothing for a man like Milan to pay attention to. Nothing at all. She exhaled deeply and trudged back out, not daring to tell Vanessa what she had been doing instead of relieving her bladder.

A large and rather rowdy group of string players had colonised the far corner of the bar, bonding over their pint glasses. Milan sat at the end of a cushioned bench, engrossed in conversation with the pretty-boy cellist.

"I'll wait here," said Vanessa, maintaining a position by the door that would aid a quick escape. "Just hand it over. No eye contact. And get out of there."

"Yes, Captain," said Lydia with a salute and a giggle. "Cover me. I'm going in."

Milan did not notice her at first until, one by one, the other members of the group broke off their conversations to stare at her. She removed the packet from her handbag and held it out.

"Your string," she said, her tone noticeably mutinous.

"Ah." Milan turned round and sent a beaming smile in her direction, a deadly weapon in the armoury of seduction. "Good girl."

Lydia almost growled.

He took the packet and stowed it in a jacket pocket before turning back to her.

"My change?"

Lydia's fist closed around the few coins.

"Don't I get commission?" she found herself saying. "It's cold out there. And wet."

Milan raised his eyebrows, tilting his head to one side in curious scrutiny. Lydia wished she looked a little less like a drowned rat crossed with a fishwife, but she held her ground.

"Commission, huh? Okay."

He made his friends shift up the bench until a small space became available beside him, then he patted the cushion.

"Sit down. I buy you a drink."

"No, I didn't mean…"

The roguish glint in his eye stripped the steel plating from her resolve. *Milan Kaspar offered to buy me a drink. I could have a drink with Milan Kaspar.*

"Come on. What do you like? Wine? Vodka? I'll buy it for you. As a thank you."

The steel plating was gone and now the core was melting. The curve of his lips, the way the smile accentuated his cheekbones, the lock of hair falling in one eye…

"Lydia!"

It was Vanessa, a long way behind, hissing to her, waving her gloved hand furiously.

"No. Thank you," she said, dropping the coins on the table.

Milan raised a hand to cup his ear, as if straining to catch her words.

"What's that I heard? It wasn't a no, was it?"

"Yes."

"Yes? Then come and sit down."

"I mean yes, it was a no." Lydia's voice grew shrill and flustered. "No!"

"You're frozen," crooned Milan, reaching out and taking one of her icy hands. "*Che gelida manina!* Come and get warm, *miláčku.*"

Lydia's vigorous shake of the head transferred to the whole of her body. Her pelvis twisted in panic as she wrenched her hand out of his.

"I said no. I have to go," she blurted, turning and half running while the going was good, hating herself for looking an idiot in front of her new colleagues, who were guffawing behind her.

"Oh, my God!" exclaimed Vanessa, hustling her outside into the frozen wastes of Westminster. "You said no to Milan. Is that the sound of a mould breaking I can hear? Come on, let's get to Starbucks. I'd kill for a mochaccino right now."

"He called me something." Lydia shivered. "Sounded like 'milch cow'."

"Heaven help you." Vanessa held open the door of the coffee shop. "You're next."

Come and get warm, miláčku.

Lydia woke up with the words echoing in her ears in Milan's velvet-clad accent. He might be off limits in her professional life, but her fantasy life was a different matter. Lydia slid her fingers down, found the warm split between her thighs, her clit swollen and bursting to be touched after a night of broken dreams featuring Milan's bowing elbow and devilish smile.

Alternative reality changed the previous evening's disastrous encounter so that her 'no' became a 'yes'. She sat down beside him and he slipped an arm around her, drawing her close, closer, as close as could be until he held her against him, her ear rubbing his shoulder so that she drew his warmth into her body. Then his fingertips, sensitive but strong, on her cheek, then his lips on hers, then the pub whirling away from them while they kissed.

His hands inside her shirt—the parka having long since dissolved—exploring her, caressing her skin, finding her breasts, laying her down…

Then they were out of the pub, in his bed, which would smell of him and his Eastern European manliness, and he had tumbled her in his rumpled sheets and they were naked.

He was playful, pouncing on her, nipping and snapping at her neck, slapping her thighs, pinning her wrists, his hair flicking over her face. She moaned as he impaled her on his cock…oh.

Retracting her fingers, Lydia sat up, hot, bothered and cross. He was a sleazy serial seducer. Why would she fantasise about that?

She lay back down and pulled one of her standard fantasies from the mental masturbation bookshelf instead. The one about the Saxon warrior spanking her with his sword would have to do. No Milan. Just pure Saxon man, overpowering her with the power of his arm-ringed biceps and throwing her over his knee. Better. Much better.

It was no use though. As her pleasure built and her release approached, Mr Saxon's arm rings disappeared, his sword turned to a violin bow, and by the time she dissolved into that final moment of bliss, Milan was back. Frustrations released, she headed for the shower.

But why did she use her most luxurious shampoo and shower gel, and why did she spritz on so much of her white jasmine and mint cologne afterwards?

She frowned at herself in the mirror as she tried to trick her long, straight brown hair into looking voluminous. Nothing worked, so she resorted to her usual ponytail. Maybe contacts… No. She put her glasses on so adamantly that she almost bent the right wire.

She was not going to attract Milan's attention. She was not going to attract Milan's attention. Rinse and repeat till fade.

"Lydia."

So much for not attracting his attention, she thought, jumping a little when he beckoned her over the minute she entered the rehearsal room. He must have been waiting for her. The idea made her shudder with unwelcome excitement.

"I have a name now, then," she said, all bravado. "Not 'new girl' any more?"

Milan smirked and looked down at his violin for a moment.

"Yesterday was an interesting day," he said. "In the way of the Chinese proverb. I had a lot on my mind. I was rude. I apologise. Can you forgive me?"

Oh, fuck, don't be nice. How am I supposed to resist you if you're nice?

"It's okay," she found herself saying. "Let's forget about it."

"Yes, let's," he said eagerly, leaning down to her eye level. "So you let me buy you a drink, yes? After the rehearsal?"

"Oh, um..." She looked around for Vanessa, who was nowhere to be seen. To say no would be churlish, and besides...a drink with Milan Kaspar... "Yes, that would be nice. Thanks."

His smile was genuine and as bright as the strip lights overhead.

"Great! That's great. I look forward to it."

Lydia put down her violin case and skipped to the back of the hall to hang up her coat and scarf. Vanessa was there, pulling off her beret.

"Oh God, oh God, oh God," squeaked Lydia. "Milan just asked me out."

Vanessa turned to her with a pained expression.

"And you said...?"

"Yes! What? He asked nicely. He wasn't being an arrogant git, honestly."

Vanessa sighed.

"It's so easy for him. Fish in a barrel."

"Oh, Vanessa, don't be like that. It's only a drink. We have to work together—we might as well be friendly."

"Just watch him. He's a predator. It won't stop at a drink, believe me."

"Yeah, but you've warned me. Forewarned is forearmed and all that."

"You don't know exactly what you're up against. Your puny cardboard shield versus his nuclear arsenal of seduction—let's say I don't fancy your chances, love."

"Wow. Nuclear arsenal of seduction."

The phrase and its implication—that Lydia was directly in the firing line—shouldn't have pleased her, but it did. She was intensely flattered at the idea that anyone could consider her worthy of pursuit by such a famous super-stud as Milan Kaspar. She was about to reassure Vanessa once more that she would keep her head clear and her knickers on when the tapping of a music stand called them to order and they scuttled to their chairs.

Milan was a good conductor, if a little imperious and impatient, and the rehearsal glided by like a harmonious dream for Lydia. He worked them hard enough that she didn't have time to daydream about what might come next, and by the time five o'clock rolled around, her bowing arm was tired and her mind full of music.

She waited, growing pinker and pinker at all the behind-the-hand whispering, while the rest of the orchestra left the hall and Milan indulged in some post-rehearsal chat with the other string players. Vanessa hung around for a while, seemingly wondering whether to stay or go, but eventually she took her beret and flounced off.

"Okay, ready?"

Milan turned to her and offered a gallant forearm, which she took.

His bowing arm. I am touching it. Her fingers rested lightly on the cool white cotton of his shirtsleeve as he walked her over to the cloakroom. He helped her on with her coat then wound her scarf gently around her neck, disarming her for a moment when he ducked his face into the soft wool.

"It smells like you," he said, coming up for air.

"Ah." Lydia caught her breath while Milan shrugged on a long wool coat, tailored to fit his tall, elegant figure and show it to its fullest advantage. Scarf and leather gloves on, he looked down at Lydia's hands.

"No gloves," he scolded. "You need to protect your hands. The cold will chap them."

"Oh, I usually just put them in my pockets."

"No good. Here."

He took Lydia's hands in his, clasping them in the smooth leather, leading her out of the door like that and into the windy early evening.

Every car and bus that passed made Lydia's stomach flip with the thought that everyone could see her walking along the street, hand in hand with Milan Kaspar.

"Is that his new girlfriend?" they might ask each other. "Did he dump that TV presenter for her?"

They wouldn't understand it, of course—a glorious, golden glamour-puss replaced by a mousy little music geek. But their love was beyond understanding...

Hold on, Lydia. Get a grip. Love? You idiot.

The Delius Arms was blessedly warm and cosy, but Lydia was almost disappointed that the brief walk in the knife-edged cold was over when Milan dropped her hands and indicated a table in the corner.

"What do you like? Red wine?"

"Actually, a hot chocolate might be nice. I'm frozen."

"Hot chocolate? No. I buy you red wine."

Lydia shrugged and went to sit down, stowing her violin case under the table and staring at her hands. They had just been held by Milan Kaspar. They looked no different—a little red and raw from the cold, but essentially the same Lydia Foster hands that had been playing the violin for the eighteen years since she started school. She tried to keep them away from anything that might rub the Milan-ness off them, putting them up to her nostrils to try to trace the faint scent of leather, but it had been too cold outside and they smelt of nothing much.

He brought over the drinks—red wine for her and something brown in a balloon glass for him.

"What's that?"

"Brandy. I need to get warm. Your winters are cold, but not as cold as the winters back home. We always had a bottle of brandy in the house."

"Back home in the Czech Republic, you mean?"

"That's right. It wasn't called that when I lived there. It was Czechoslovakia, and before that Bohemia."

"How lovely. A true Bohemian. Do you fit the description?"

Milan smiled over his brandy glass.

"I suppose I do. I'm an artist and my hair is a bit longer than most men's. Bohemian by nationality and by disposition. How about you?"

"Oh, well, I'm not from anywhere exciting, like you. Boring old Guildford. I live in London now, though. London's exciting."

"Yes, it is. I like it."

"Do you ever miss your homeland?"

"All the time. Every day."

"Would you ever go back?"

"Why are we talking about me? That is not why I invited you here."

Lydia was beguiled by Milan's intense look, head cocked to one side.

"Oh… Why…did you? Invite me here, I mean."

Unnervingly, Milan did not reply, but simply let his eyes rest on her face as if seeking some higher truth in it.

"Take off your glasses," he said at last.

Lydia obeyed, laying them on the table.

"Are you going to ask me to let down my hair?" she asked with a nervous laugh.

"Why not? Go on."

With shaking fingers she loosened her ponytail, letting her straight, mid-brown hair fall freely over her shoulders.

"Now you are not the mouse any more. You are very pretty. Why do you hide? And those clothes — fleeces are for middle-aged people who like to ramble in the countryside."

"Oh, I'm not very good at shopping." Lydia hid her flush with a deep gulp of the wine. "Takes up too much rehearsal time."

"You are unworldly. And you don't wear makeup. You don't need to." He leant forward, so suddenly that Lydia spilled a little of the wine on her derided fleece. "Are you scared, Lydia?"

"Scared? Of what?"

"Of male attention. Men. Sex. Love."

"No, no, of course not!"

"I hope not. Fear makes a poor musician. A good violinist is open, with herself and others."

"Is this some kind of interview? I must say, I don't think my appearance or personal relationships are really—"

"Relevant? Yes, they are. I'll get you another drink, wait there."

He gave Lydia a few moments of recovery time while he bought another round. She wanted to ask him to get her something non-alcoholic, but she knew he would refuse. She could not work out how she felt. Intimidated? A little. Infatuated? A lot. Imperilled? Most definitely. He had called her pretty. And the way he'd *looked* at her...

The same look set her to fluttering when he returned and put down the drinks.

"Show me your hands," he said, taking them in his before she had a chance. "Good violinist's hands. But small. Maybe you couldn't play the piano, eh?"

Lydia was too transfixed on Milan's own famous hands to reply. The fingers that plucked the strings were stroking her knuckles. She never wanted it to end.

"Why do you play, Lydia?" he asked softly.

"Because I must," she said without thinking.

"Exactly. Exactly so."

He nodded at her, approving of the sentiment.

"I think we'll work well together." He dropped her hands abruptly so that they fell to the table with a thunk. "Drink your wine. I will buy you dinner. Is a nice place around the corner."

Chapter Three

The meal seemed to Lydia to pass in a golden haze. Buoyed by the wine and the intoxication of Milan's attention, she floated through two hours that passed like minutes. Milan wanted to know every detail of her musical education and tastes; then he moved on to more personal matters.

"Have you ever been in love?" he asked, while they waited for the bill.

She drummed her fingertips on the rim of her empty glass, knowing she was heading for dangerous rocks, but powerless to steer her craft away from them.

"I don't know," she said.

"So that's a no." Milan tutted. "You would know if you had."

"I suppose."

"So who was the lucky man?"

"Wha—?"

"Your first. Your first lover. Was he worthy of you?"

"I don't know!"

"You don't know who your first lover was? Lydia, I did not think you were such a bad girl!"

"No, no, the worthy thing. For God's sake, Milan! Of course I know who it was. But it doesn't matter. I'm not with him any more. That all ended ages ago."

"He wasn't worthy of you, then."

"He was all right!"

"Don't tell me he was all right. I am jealous of him."

"Oh, you're not!"

"I am."

A waiter appeared and Milan turned his attention to paying the bill, leaving Lydia to try to focus her eyes and pour a deep drink from the water jug.

"I like the way you say my name," he said, whirling back to her before she was ready. "Say it again."

"Milan. I didn't even realise it was a name until I heard of you. Thought it was an Italian city."

"I think it is Czech version of Miles. I don't know. I like Lydia. Pretty name for a pretty girl."

The waiter brought their coats, and Milan helped Lydia into hers again, though this time he lingered over the buttons, breathing into her ear as he fastened them from behind.

Lydia swayed on unsteady feet, leaning back into Milan's welcoming body. He made a sound, between a growl and a sigh, that travelled straight down her ear and into her crotch.

One arm around her shoulder, he escorted her out into the shocking cold of the street.

"It's *freezing!*" she exclaimed, as the wind bit into her wine-warmed cheeks.

"I can warm you up if you like."

"Oh?" She turned her face up to him, knowing what was coming, wanting and dreading it, ready to be doomed.

He bundled her against him, slid a hand to the back of her head and guided her into a world away from the bitter city pavement, a world of hot breath, firm lips and exploring tongues. Lydia's body and soul flooded with blissful desire as he opened and closed his leather-gloved fingers on the soft flesh at the nape of her neck, probing through her hair. He felt like nothing she had experienced before; he felt like passion. *This is passion, the thing I've only felt for music before.* Innumerable buses and taxis had rumbled past before he released her from his savage caress, leaving her blinking, lips aflame, in the sleet she had not noticed until now.

"What now?" she stammered.

"Come with me."

They took a taxi to the Barbican, a place where Lydia had enjoyed many an evening of top-class musical entertainment.

"We're going to a concert?" she asked, puzzled.

"No," said Milan, helping her out of the cab. "I live here."

"In the Barbican? Wow! In one of those huge flats?" She pointed up at the floor-to-ceiling windows, many of them lit up like Christmas. She had often wandered around the fountains during concert intervals, imagining the sophisticated scenes taking place inside the exclusive condominiums. Now it seemed she was going to star in one of those sophisticated scenes herself. *Except I'm the least sophisticated person in the world. Unlike him.*

The thought made her uneasy, but it didn't trouble her for long, vanishing as soon as Milan took her arm and led her towards the looming complex.

She wanted to ask a million questions but she didn't dare, in case any of the answers broke this breathless spell. *Going home with Milan Kaspar. It won't be a one-night stand. It can't be.*

In the elevator, he held her face and kissed her again, all the way up to the top floor, unzipping her parka with his free hand and sliding it inside, looking for a way under her fleece.

His palm had found her bare stomach by the time the doors opened, and they half fell along the corridor, still kissing, until Milan pushed Lydia up against a wall, causing her to drop her violin case with a thump. Her fleece was up over her bra and Milan's thumbs were on their way inside the cups when a door opened.

"At last," said a laconic, Russian-accented voice.

Lydia shrieked into Milan's mouth, wriggling to find an escape that didn't come. Why was he still doing this, right in front of Evgeny the cellist? And what was Evgeny the cellist doing here, anyway? Were they neighbours?

"Put her down, Milan. At least, for now."

Reluctantly, Milan pulled the fleece back down and withdrew from the embrace, pulling Lydia onward by the wrist to where Evgeny stood, one eyebrow raised, arms folded.

"What's happening?" whimpered Lydia, suddenly very sober.

"You've passed the first test," Milan informed her, his voice terse. "You're going to be vetted. And, if you pass the vetting, you're going to be initiated."

"*What?*" Her yelp of protest preceded her into the huge, luxurious living room—then it died in her throat. For Evgeny's presence was the least of her problems. Sitting in ranks on the sofas and chairs were five of her colleagues in the First Violins, plus a select few Second Violins, Violas and Cellos.

"Twelve good men and true," said Milan, drumming his fingertips against the nape of her neck in an effort to calm her. "Or rather, nine men, two women...and you."

"What's going on?"

"This, Lydia, is the secret heart of the Westminster Symphony Orchestra. You have a chance to influence and change the direction of the orchestra, if you agree to join us."

"Join you? What is this? Like...like a musical version of the Freemasons?"

Milan chuckled, as did several of the other players.

"Yes, I suppose it's a good analogy. We are all good musicians, strong musicians, who are tired of being told what we should do by conductors. We know our jobs. We know music. If we succeed, I will eventually be made conductor-leader, as some orchestras already have. What's to stop me conducting the orchestra from the violin section? I won't be the first. I certainly won't be the last."

"This is why you were being weird with Josh Clayton yesterday?"

"In a word, yes. What do you say? Are you in?"

"You said something about vetting."

"Well, vetting is a formality. If you want to join us, you can join us. But we don't accept people with closed minds or repressed attitudes."

"What do you mean? And what about this...initiation?"

She turned to Milan, full of distress at having been tricked into his arms. It had all been a ploy to get her here, to join this half-baked plot. She wanted to slap him.

"You're a sensual woman, Lydia," crooned Milan, reaching out to stroke her arm. "Just like Gina...and Karin..." He waved towards the other two women in the room, who smiled invitingly. "Gina, tell Lydia here about your initiation."

Gina laughed throatily. "I sucked a lot of cock that night."

"Stop!" Lydia, shaking, wrenched herself free of Milan.

"No, no, be open-minded, listen," he urged.

"And I had a lot of orgasms," continued Gina. "It was the best night of my life. All the sex I ever wanted, the way I wanted it. We are all good friends, Lydia. It's a mutually satisfying arrangement. No need for all that dating angst—great sex on tap, whenever you want it."

"I don't want that! I want love!"

Lydia, feeling like an idiot as various players rolled their eyes at each other, turned around, looking for an escape.

"I wanted you!" she raged at Milan. "But I was stupid to want you. You don't care about anybody."

He reached out to halt her, but she kicked his shin with some force and ran past Evgeny and out of the door, faster than she knew she could move.

Outside by the fountain, she sat down and wept, cursing her credulity. How could she have thought Milan's interest in her genuine? How could she have been such a fool?

She sobbed in the sleet for a long time, until the rest of the players had all left the apartment and drifted in pairs and threes towards the Tube station, then she stared bleakly up at the starless sky and let the cold claw her face to ribbons.

"Oh, *fuck!*" she suddenly lamented through chattering teeth. "My fucking violin!"

She had left it in the apartment.

She would have to go back.

She rang and rang at the doorbell until Milan's sleepy voice came across the intercom.

"Yes?"

"It's Lydia. You have my violin."

"Ah. Come on up."

The front door to his apartment was ajar and she wandered into the hallway, spotting her violin case immediately. It was propped up next to a large pot plant.

There was no sign of Milan. Should she just leave? Was he in bed?

A strange moaning noise came from the living room. Lydia, wanting to postpone her return to the frozen wastelands of London after dark, tiptoed to the interconnecting door, which was half open.

Peering through the crack, she had to suppress her instinctive sharp breath.

Evgeny and Milan sat together on a sofa, both perfectly naked, while Evgeny's pretty head rested against Milan's chest. Milan stroked his hair and whispered words she couldn't hear, while his fist moved slowly but firmly along the length of Evgeny's cock.

Evgeny moved his head up and the pair began to kiss, deeply.

Lydia couldn't move. What was going to happen? Milan sped up and Evgeny began to make little helpless noises until the kiss was broken. Milan sank his teeth into Evgeny's shoulder and Evgeny cried out, his cock expelling snakes of pearlescent ejaculate over his abdomen and thighs.

"Come in and get warm, Lydia," drawled Milan, without looking away from Evgeny.

Completely at sea, she stepped into the room. How should she feel about this? It was so far beyond her experience that she had no frame of reference to consult. But then the entire evening had been the same. Perhaps she should abandon her expectations of the world here and now.

"You should have told me," she said haltingly. "That you were gay. Why did you ask me out if…if…"

Milan lifted his head from Evgeny's neck and stared at Lydia, his lips quirked upwards.

"I'm not gay," he said.

"What? Then what…?"

"Even you must have heard of bisexuality?"

What do you mean, 'even me'?

"Of course, but…but…"

"But what?"

"It's just something people say, isn't it? I've never known anyone that actually…did."

Milan sighed, sat up and patted the sofa next to him.

"Come and sit here," he said, the tone so like an order that Lydia obeyed unthinkingly. She caught Evgeny's flicker of detached amusement. It looked a lot like contempt, but she made an effort to ignore it.

Milan reached forward and poured her a glass of iced water from a jug on the nearby table. She drank gratefully, already afflicted with the fuzzy head and thick tongue of a hangover.

"Now listen, Lydia. I get the idea that you have some traditional views when it comes to relationships, am I right? Boy meets girl, they live monogamously ever after, et cetera."

"I'm not homophobic, if that's what you're implying."

"It isn't. If I thought you were homophobic I'd never have invited you here, clear?"

"Yes. Clear. Good."

"But am I right?"

"I suppose it's what I've been brought up to believe. I'll meet someone special, yada yada."

"Okay. Well, I believe that there are lots of special people in this world. I don't see the value of limiting yourself to just one."

"You want to have your cake and eat it, you mean?" said Lydia snippily.

"Yes." Milan smiled broadly. "I like cake. Lots of cake. I know you don't like shopping, but what do you do, Lydia, when you see two fleeces that you like? Both so comfortable, so...fleecy. But slightly different colours."

Evgeny giggled. Lydia pursed her lips.

"Don't tease me."

"I'm sorry. But is there a law that forbids you buying both? Come on! Have both! Live a little! Buy two fleeces instead of one!"

"Milan!"

Evgeny was laughing outright now, pouring himself a glass of water.

"That's a crappy analogy," said Lydia. "I don't commit myself to my purchases like I would to a lover."

"Good. Because I think you should certainly be unfaithful to that fleece."

"Oh, shut *up!* So you're saying you would never be faithful to a partner?"

Milan touched barely-there fingers to the back of Lydia's head, raking them lightly through her hair.

"No, Lydia, I'm not saying that. I'm saying our concepts of fidelity might not be the same. I love lots of people. Lots of special people. Evgeny is one of them. I think you could be another."

She shivered as his fingertips brushed the nape of her neck.

"If it was just you…" she whispered.

"You can't tie me down," he murmured into her ear. "And, in return, I won't tie you down. Well, unless you ask me to. Bondage can be fun…"

"You aren't taking any of this seriously, are you?"

"Love and sex are too important to take seriously."

She turned her face to him. His eyes were infinite, misty-blue, seeking out her core. She had thought her code of sexual ethics was strong… but where was it now?

"You really think I'm special?"

"Don't you? You are, Lydia. You should know it. I could show you how special you are."

His lips were gentle on her forehead, then the tip of her nose.

"And…Evgeny?"

"He wants you too. We talked about you all last night. We would treat you so well… We could show you *how* well. Now, if you like."

He had captured her ear with his mouth, and was sending hot waves of desire down its curling shell and deep into her groin.

How would it hurt…just to let him do what he wanted…?

She offered no resistance when he drew her, slowly and sweetly, into a hungry kiss. Encompassing her with his arm, he drew her onto his lap so that her jeans-clad bottom nestled on his bare thighs. She felt him harden beneath her. His hands and his tongue felt so perfect that she forgot Evgeny, who was sitting beside them, watching, right up to the point where Milan bit her lower lip gently and moved his mouth to her ear.

"I'm going to take that bloody fleece off."

"Oh!" she whimpered, suddenly aware of greedy black eyes drinking her in from the other end of the sofa. "But Evgeny...?"

"Shh. You've had sex with one man before, yes?"

"Yes."

"Haven't you ever wondered how much better it could be with two?"

"Well...maybe. But as a fantasy. It all seemed too difficult in real life."

"No, it's easy. It will be easy. And you will never want to go back, once you have had two men want you and lust after you and give you all their love and attention. I promise you, *miláčku*." While he spoke, he eased the fleece up and over her head. Spellbound, she raised her arms and let him pull it off, revealing her plain white cotton bra.

"So pretty." Evgeny's first words were appreciative, and Lydia flicked her eyes over to him, blushing.

"Oh yes," crooned Milan, bending to kiss each of the pale slopes of her breasts in turn. "Too pretty to keep to myself. I want to see you kissing Evgeny. I want to watch you together."

Lydia hesitated, but then a rush of blood to the head made the decision for her. She had come too far to turn back now—there seemed no way she could simply put the fleece back on and flee. She was entangled in the seductive threads of Milan's erotic imagination, and it seemed, at that moment, the only place she wanted to be.

"That's what you want?" she asked huskily.

"Oh, yes. It's what I want."

She dismounted from Milan's lap and handed herself over to Evgeny, kneeling at his side, while he rose to his own knees and gathered her into an embrace. He felt different from Milan—he was slenderer and bonier, and his lips were fuller. Those sweeping eyelashes tickled against her skin as the kiss continued. He smelt of a lovely, unfamiliar aftershave mixed with his own male essence, now dried onto him.

"That's nice." Milan's commentary came from over her shoulder. "I can only see your back, but I like the way those jeans fit your arse. Good and tight. In fact..."

Lydia, lost in Evgeny's kiss, hardly reacted when Milan shimmied up behind her and placed his hands on her cotton-covered breasts, kneading and tweaking them while he nipped at the back of her neck. She felt his cock pushing at the seat of her jeans, trying to forge a path between her tightly denimed buttocks.

With one set of male lips on her mouth and another on her neck, Lydia felt her inhibitions dissolve. Milan teased her nipples while Evgeny held her by the hips, pushing her back against his lover's body. When Evgeny reached for her jeans zipper, she was well beyond the point of no return. She mutely acquiesced to the slow exposure of her plain cotton briefs, enjoying the way Milan slid his palm down over her bottom and squeezed.

He nudged her knees up so he could pull the jeans all the way off, then batted Evgeny away and took possession of Lydia's mouth again with his, tongue delving deep. Evgeny fiddled with her bra straps, freeing her breasts for more lavish attention. His touch did not have quite the finesse of Milan's, but all the same he stroked her nipples to devastating effect until she was moaning into the violinist's mouth and squirming between the two hard bodies that held her so firmly in place.

Milan released her lips and murmured, "What do you want first?"

"Hmm?"

"So many ways to play a trio... What movement should we start with? *Allegro vivace?* Or *adagio?*"

"Milan, I..."

"It's okay. I know you're shy. And this is an amazing thing for you. You want me to direct?"

"Please. You're a good conductor."

He stroked her cheek, smiling fondly.

"Thank you," he whispered.

He glanced over at the cellist, and Lydia turned to look too, noting that Evgeny held his semi-erect cock in his hand while he worked at bringing it to full engorgement.

"Too soon after the last time?"

Evgeny nodded.

"Okay. Lydia, would you like to taste him? I can vouch for the flavour—very nice." Milan nuzzled Lydia's neck and held her around the base of her ribcage as he made the dark-toned suggestion. "He is nearly ready for you—he just needs a little oral encouragement."

Lydia looked into Milan's eyes, seeking something like reassurance, something she could trust. She saw sparks of fire, urgent desire. Was it enough? She thought it would be.

She bent forwards and knelt in front of Evgeny, taking his cock in her hands first, feeling its length and girth, before breathing over the glans. Milan took hold of her waist, keeping her balanced as she dipped her head lower. Evgeny cried out in rapture at the first contact of her wet lips against his half-mast prick and a frisson of tenderness overcame Lydia. Bringing her tongue forward to curl around the moistened tip, she felt a bloom of pride at the way his flesh firmed in her mouth, quickly and eagerly.

Meanwhile, Milan tugged at the waistband of her knickers, helping them crest the ridge of her buttocks and slide down her thighs, over her knees and down until she was nude. Naked in front of two men, both of whom expected to make her come.

She clamped her thighs together, shivering at the knowledge of her exposure, but Milan made deft work of parting her legs for his inspection, and he spoke in a low, masterful tone as she sucked and licked at Evgeny's enlarging cock.

"You have a lovely pussy, Lydia," he said. She moaned over her mouthful as Milan bent closer, his hair brushing the back of her thighs so that they goosepimpled, and his breath warmed her defenceless sex. "It looks so sweet and pink. I can't wait to eat it."

He spread her parted lips wider with his thumbs and she wriggled. Evgeny placed a hand in her hair, perhaps afraid that she might lose her rhythm if Milan distracted her too much. The gesture reminded her to attend to her task, and she stilled, letting Milan explore the relief map of her vulva and clit.

"Very wet," he observed, gathering a coating of her copious juices from each crease. "You like giving head, Lydia?"

She made an inarticulate reply, sucking all the harder.

"You know what I like? I like a nice juicy clit to lick. I've got one here, just right for me. Swollen and ripe. I'm going to lick it until you scream. Are you ready?"

For reasons she couldn't articulate, Lydia was suddenly scared of the intense sensation she knew Milan's tongue would bring. Would it be too much to bear? Would she end up screaming or crying or embarrassing herself in some other way?

He appeared to sense her wave of reservation, for he removed his fingers from her sticky core and patted her rump for a moment, the gentle rhythm of it settling her once more, whilst the sudden absence of his wicked doings between her legs proved too cruel to endure. She circled her hips, indicating that she wanted him back there.

"It's okay," he said. "It's all for you. We want to make you happy. If you aren't happy, we will stop."

She pushed out her bottom, desperate now to feel Milan's honeyed tongue on her most intimate parts. His breath was enough to set off a million tiny bubbles of lust in her stomach. Her clit felt heavy and huge, waiting there between her lips like the clapper of a bell, wanting to be rung.

He growled, and she felt the vibrations from his throat all the way through her. Her pussy tensed and contracted, then his tongue was there, hot and wet, muscular and tender, lapping her up as if she were the most delicious morsel on earth.

He pulled her bum cheeks apart with his thumbs, holding her widespread and vulnerable so that there could be no escape from the plundering strokes of that tyrant tongue. Her legs shook and she began to choke on Evgeny's cock, losing control of her actions. The cellist drew his shaft slowly out of her mouth and stroked her hair. Her job was done and now she was reaping the rewards, gasping helplessly into the sofa cushion while Milan continued to lick her out with thorough expertise.

"You will come soon," hissed Evgeny, tugging at her hair as if it were a leash.

Milan worked two fingers into her cunt and she began to spasm, yelping into the cushion, helpless beneath the onslaught of her idol's ministrations.

She knew that Evgeny was watching her most intimate moment, and that Milan was chuckling in triumph, but this made the sweetness of it all the more intense and she let herself be taken into two pairs of arms and kissed all over her face and neck.

"You see how it can be?" whispered Milan.

"I think...I'm starting to..."

Two cocks prodded urgently at her hips and she wondered cloudily what was going to be done about that. Milan would have a plan, she thought.

"I think it might be a little too soon for anything too crazy," murmured Milan, ostensibly to Evgeny. "But we can save the more advanced stuff for later. We have time. Lots of time."

"So how do you want to do this?" Evgeny asked.

"Shall we just...hey, Lydia. You should have a say in this. Are you capable of speech yet?"

"Nn hnn."

"I want to make love to you. Evgeny wants to make love to you. Do you think you could take both of us tonight? Or if you just want one we can work around that."

"I'm not sure." Lydia flicked wide eyes up to Milan. She wanted him. She hoped he understood. Evgeny was handsome, a bonus, but if he decided to leave right now it would be fine by her. "I'm not sure how it would make me feel..."

"You want to play safe? That's not a problem. So you and me tonight? Is it okay if Evgeny watches?"

"Umm...yes." Was it? She looked up at Evgeny's stormy dark eyes. Yes. He could come into the bedroom with them.

"That's good. We want him to learn what turns you on."

Milan stood abruptly, extending a hand to Lydia.

"Okay, bedtime," he said.

Chapter Four

When she stood, warmed and naked against his body, he pulled her to him as if they were about to dance. He kissed her hard before twirling her back out, then led her to a room beyond the huge, plate-glass-windowed living room. Evgeny followed, his shoulders sloping a little as if he were aggrieved, bringing the brandy decanter and glass with him.

He slumped into an armchair in the corner and poured himself a drink. Milan and Lydia came back together, circling and kissing across the deep-pile carpet until they fell upon the huge, circular bed with its black satin sheets and piles of pillows.

"Oh, my God," gasped Lydia with a giggle. "This is like the Playboy mansion. You have a mirror on the ceiling!"

"I am a famous playboy—what do you expect?" Milan settled his long, lean body in beside her, propping his weight on one elbow. He traced feathery patterns across her abdomen and chest with his fingers while he smouldered down at her. "You can see what I am doing to you."

Lydia, staring up at her reflection, saw her body in a different light. She rarely looked at herself but now, flushed with desire, wantonly naked, she thought she looked lush and ready for ravishment. If it was obvious to her, it must be doubly so to Milan...and Evgeny.

She watched his fingers for a while before moving her gaze back to Milan's face.

"So that's what we're doing?" she asked, suddenly insecure. "Playing?"

"We play for a living, my dear. Playing is a serious business. Let's give ourselves to pleasure."

He bent to kiss her lips and his kiss brought the gift of forgetfulness, of oblivion, sweeping away her doubts and fears.

He pushed his fingertips inside her and she opened up for them, rubbing her leg against Milan's.

"Do you want me to take you now?" The words drifted over her skin.

"Are you...do you have something?"

"It's okay. Evgeny!"

His imperious tone brought the cellist rushing across the room to hand over a condom from the dresser. Lydia watched him from the corner of her eye, noting the curious fascination in his face. He did not return to the chair but remained at the end of the bed, holding his cock in his hand and watching Milan apply the rubber.

"He can stay there?" asked Milan gently, lowering himself to crouch over Lydia, millimetres of humid air between their pelvises.

"Yeah." His cock was lined up and ready. She was wet and pinned down beneath the legendary Milan Kaspar, about to be fucked by the greatest orchestral violinist in the world. She took a moment to drink it all in, then whispered, "Please...Milan."

He seated himself swiftly, filling her. Her head swam and she moaned, wondering why it had never felt as good as this before. What was he doing that was different? Or was it just *him*, his magic touch, his artist's consciousness?

Lydia brought a leg up over his hip and wrapped it around his buttocks, keeping him close to her. She held his shoulders, fingertips pressing into his firm flesh as he began, slowly at first, to thrust.

"You feel so good, Lydia, so tight," he told her.

And the thought that this information could also be for Evgeny's benefit made her moan aloud.

She looked up, seeing her face with its dewy blush and Milan's lean back and powerful shoulders looming over it. God, what a sight that was. She couldn't tear her eyes away, mesmerised by each back and forth motion of his thighs and bottom, the gluteal muscles tightening and releasing as Milan's expert fucking took her higher and higher.

"How does it feel?" he panted, gathering speed.

"So good, oh, so good. Keep going, I've never had it like this..."

He growled and thrust harder, holding her by her hair so that trillions of endorphins sparked across her scalp.

"You'll get it like this, oh yes, every day, every night, believe it."

"Oh, God." She began to whimper, the reflection on the ceiling blurring.

"We were right about her, Evgeny, she loves it."

"I can see that."

His rich Russian-accented voice, with its edge of dry humour, pushed her closer to the edge. She was being fucked and watched. He was taking notes for when he would fuck her himself. It was a monumental thought.

"Love it, Lydia, love it. We want to give it to you... We want to make you come..."

Milan's fervent mutterings did the trick and she came, too overwhelmed to remember to look at herself in the mirror, twisting and turning beneath Milan's strong body. He let himself go, releasing inside her, whipping his hair across his face.

He reared up, shoulders back, eyes alight, drawing a huge breath before breaking into laughter.

Lydia opened her eyes again, in time to see Evgeny join them on the bed, stroking his cock with breakneck speed. She stared from him to Milan and back again, squealing as warm semen jetted onto her belly and breasts, to her lover's very obvious delight.

Later, lying cradled against Milan while Evgeny sponged off every last trace of semen with loving care, following up each dab with a kiss on the same spot, Lydia drew a coherent thread from the spinning wheel of her mind.

"Can this really work?"

"Of course it can," said Milan, his chin resting on her head. "Don't think about it. Just let it happen."

"Just let it happen," she repeated, smiling at Evgeny, who, for the first time, smiled back at her.

Upon arrival at the afternoon rehearsal, Lydia was aware of a buzz in the air.

She was also aware of a throbbing between her legs and a tight knot of excitement in her chest, but she tried her level best to ignore those.

Hanging up her coat, she scanned the groups of gossiping musicians for Milan, finding him amongst some string players, holding forth with a gleam in his eye.

She felt a pang in her heart. Milan Kaspar, her intense, charismatic lover. She needed somebody to pass the smelling salts but, instead, Vanessa appeared at her elbow, whispering conspiratorially.

"I hope you aren't going to tell me he got you into bed," she said.

"Umm...I'm not going to tell you that," said Lydia, but she was pretty sure her blush was broadcasting the news on her behalf.

"*Lydia!*"

"Damn it, Vanessa, he's impossible to resist."

Vanessa sighed.

"I know," she said. "Believe me, I know."

Lydia caught her breath. "Oh?"

But there wasn't time to elaborate. A group of important-looking people strode through the swing doors and up to the front of the hall, eliciting an expectant silence from the orchestra members, who immediately found their seats.

Lydia scurried to hers, fancying some pursed lips from the string players whose fun she had prematurely put an end to last night at Milan's apartment. They clearly had no idea she and Milan had...oh, they had...

Her drift into daydreams was halted by the tapping of a conductor's baton on the music stand at the front, wielded by one of the trustees she remembered from her interview.

She glanced down the row to Milan, who sat with his arms folded and a thunderous brow, scowling out at Lord Bicester, who was preparing to speak.

"It isn't easy," he opened, "trying to find a world-class conductor with a free schedule at a moment's notice, as I'm sure you'll understand. We, the trustees, had resigned ourselves to a long stint of guests and some broken concert engagements. But we have been immensely fortunate. Fresh from a successful run with the London Mozart Players, we have managed to snag one of the hottest young conductors around — please welcome Ms Mary-Ann McKenzie."

Lydia applauded enthusiastically, having seen and admired the new conductor's technique, but she couldn't help noticing that most of the string section's clapping was decidedly lacklustre. As for Milan, he hadn't even unfolded his arms. *How rude.*

Mary-Ann, a slender brunette in a snappy trouser suit and owlish spectacles, stepped up to the podium, smiling warmly.

"Wow," she said, pretending to be dazzled by the collective glare emanating from her new orchestra. "This is somewhere I never dreamed I'd be standing. I keep waiting to wake up and find out it's all a dream. Better than the one where all my teeth fall out, by miles."

She waited for a response, any response, but none came, though Lydia smiled sympathetically.

"Okay, well..." she continued, her cheerful façade cracking slightly. "Tough crowd! But let's move on and talk about the schedule for the first part of the year, up to Easter. We've some one-off concerts leading into spring — one at the Bridgewater Hall, another at the Barbican — then at the start of April we're off on a week's tour, going to Budapest, Vienna and finishing in Prague. It's a bit like taking coals to Newcastle with the programme, which is music about, or evoking, those particular countries and cities. We've got some Weber, some Strauss, some

Beethoven, then some Hungarian Rhapsodies, Bohemian Dances and a bit of *Má Vlast* —"

She broke off. Milan had actually stamped his foot on the floor and everyone was looking at him. Lydia wondered if he was about to explode. He was deathly pale and his lips had faded into a tight white line.

"Umm, did you want to say something, Mr Kaspar?" asked Mary-Ann politely.

He shook his head, visibly seething. "No. Carry on," he muttered.

"So...you see...there's some music from each of our tour countries...er, hang on. Lost the thread a bit. Let me think what I was going to say..."

Poor Mary-Ann battled on through the waves of hostility and indifference until her dauntless spirit petered out, and she resorted to handing out music scores and making a first rough stab at some Hungarian Rhapsodies.

With the trustees watching, the rehearsal went smoothly enough, though the atmosphere was heavier than lead. Lydia had no success in trying to meet Milan's eye, and Evgeny wasn't playing nicely either. It was as if last night had never happened.

Actually, *had* it really happened? Perhaps it hadn't, and was simply a hyper-vivid wish-fulfilment dream. Though why had she included Evgeny, and all that sitting around in the rain, if so? No, it must have happened.

At the rehearsal's end, whilst all around her packed their instruments, she made a tentative foray over to Milan.

"Are you okay?" she asked, once Mary-Ann was out of earshot.

His answer was a furious sweep of his arm, causing her to duck and totter backwards in alarm.

"Does he look okay?" said a laconic viola player. "I'd leave it, love."

She took his advice and marched to the back of the hall, swinging her violin case in ire. Bloody Milan. Sulking like a baby. Talk about taking the artistic temperament too far.

"Ignore him," confided Vanessa, grabbing her coat and scarf. "He's having an epic ego-strop. He'll come round."

"There's no excuse to be so fucking rude." Lydia was seething. "Just because they've hired another conductor – and a good one, too. What a twat. I've gone right off him." *I wish.*

"It's not just that," said Vanessa. "It's because they're doing *Má Vlast.*"

"Oh. Oh, yeah. He's from Prague, isn't he?"

They swung through the double doors together, heading out to the grim, grey street.

"Exactly. So he takes it very personally if anyone non-Czech tries to conduct Czech music. I guess that's what's bugging him the most."

"I suppose. *Má vlast* means 'my country', doesn't it? I can see how that might rile him."

"Hmm. 'Homeland'. I think he does miss his homeland."

"All the same..."

"Yes. All the same. You aren't going to carry on with him, are you, Lydia? He'll use you. He'll break your heart. He'll make you do things you'll hate yourself for."

"Is that what he did to you?"

"Yes. That's what he did to me."

They parted at the Underground station, taking different lines home. Lydia sat with her head against the dusty, padded rest and swallowed back tears all the way.

She avoided Milan the next day, deliberately going over to talk to Vanessa instead of joining the strings for a pre-rehearsal tune-up.

"He's looking at you," said Vanessa, only seconds into the conversation.

"He can look as much as he wants. Sod him."

"He's *really* looking at you. In that smouldery, bedroom-eyed Milan way."

"Let him smoulder." But Lydia had to force herself not to look.

"He's coming over."

"Shit. I don't want to talk to him, Vanessa, tell him—"

"Lydia."

His voice, right behind her, shattered every good resolution. She turned around, trying to act surprised.

"Oh. Milan." Then, after a slightly sulky pause, "Did you want something?"

"A word. Please." He gestured her away from Vanessa. She didn't dare look back at her friend, knowing disapproval would be written all over her face, but when it came to Milan there seemed to be magic in the air. The kind that put you under a spell.

She shuffled off after him, to a dark corner of the hall.

"I'm sorry," he said, bending earnestly towards her. "I didn't mean to drive you away yesterday. I was—"

"Rude? Horrible?"

"Yes." He nodded vigorously. "I know. I was angry. But not with you. Never with you."

"You were angry about the Smetana?"

"Exactly. *My* country, you know, not hers. I knew you'd understand."

"I do, in a way, but—"

"Can you forgive me? I don't deserve it, but to lose you as well as the chance to conduct... Well, it would serve me right, I guess—"

"No, no, Milan...it's okay. Really. But please don't ever treat me like that again."

"Let me make it up to you. I have tickets for *Rigoletto* at Covent Garden—the Royal Box! And for dinner afterwards. You will come, yes?"

"The Royal Box? Really?"

"Ah, when you are on TV suddenly everyone is crazy, giving you things." Milan rolled his eyes and grinned wolfishly, irresistibly.

Lydia despised herself, but her heart seemed to have cut adrift from her head and was floating dangerously out of control, drawing the rest of her in its destructive wake.

"Just you and me? Or Evgeny too?" she asked softly.

"Just you and me."

"I'd love to."

"Great. Saturday. Let's make a day of it. I'll meet you for lunch."

"Okay. Lovely."

Mary-Ann entered the hall in a beautifully-cut pinstriped suit, head down, jaw set.

"Good," breathed Milan, watching her stomping progress. "Now let's have some fun."

The rehearsal went badly. Very badly. And so did the next, and the one after that.

Lydia, watching Mary-Ann try tactic after tactic to get the orchestra on her side, felt uncomfortable and sorry for her. She started off with bluff jollying along, moved on to reason, through sarcasm, remonstration and ended, worryingly quickly, at pleading. But, no matter what she did, the tempos were all wrong, the strings shrieked rather than sang, and people persistently came in at the wrong bar, or finished the phrase in a ragged shambles. Lydia couldn't believe how easy it was for a world-class orchestra to sound like a school band. She felt ashamed of Milan and embarrassed for the Westminster Symphony and its supporters. No matter how hot she was for the first violinist, she would never approve of this strategy.

On her way to the Tube station on the Friday night before her hot date with Milan, Lydia was surprised to find herself beckoned into a coffee shop by Mary-Ann, who was sitting glumly in the window sucking up an extra-huge dose of caffeinated badness.

"Oh, hello," she said, poking her head around the door.

"Come in," said Mary-Ann. "Shut that door, for heaven's sake, you'll let that bitter wind in. Let me get you a coffee. If that's okay, I mean. Are you in a hurry?"

"No," said Lydia, perching on the neighbouring stool. "Just a long night of practicing and watching old concerts on Sky Arts for me."

"Ah, know the feeling. So, then – what's your poison?"

Mary-Ann brought Lydia a large cappuccino, plus a second extra-strong espresso for herself.

"I hope you don't mind my collaring you like this, Lydia, but I've noticed this week that you don't seem to be as 'in tune' with the string section as some, and I'm just wondering…what gives?"

Lydia felt cornered, but she couldn't help liking and respecting the forthright woman, so she took a long sip of her cappuccino and mentally put some words in as tactful an order as she could.

"I mean," Mary-Ann rattled on, almost to herself, "this is one of the world's great orchestras. But it sounds fucking awful. Is it me? Is it me, Lydia?"

"No," she said. "It's not you."

"Then what? Something's going on with Mr Milan-the-Sleb... That much I can make out. But what's his problem? Does he hate women conductors?"

"No. But he hates conductors who aren't him. Especially when they're conducting classics by Czech composers."

"Ah, right. I did wonder about the wisdom of *Má Vlast*, but the trustees insisted."

"That's at the heart of it," said Lydia, wondering how much more to reveal. "Plus it seems to be his dream to be the orchestra's leader-conductor. You've come in and scuppered that one for the time being."

"Hmm. But he's just one man, Lydia. Surely they don't *all* want to be conductors?"

"No, but they all want him to get what he wants. He has them in the palm of his hand."

"But not you?" Mary-Ann leaned a little closer, her coffee-breath drifting up to Lydia's nostrils.

"I don't really approve," said Lydia weakly. "I think he should make his case with the trustees if he wants to conduct, instead of waging war campaigns."

"The trustees don't know this goes on?"

"Oh, don't tell them!"

"Don't worry. I won't run and tell tales. But thanks for this, Lydia. I've got a handle on Milan now. I can work on it."

"Right." Lydia heaved a relieved sigh. She might not like Milan's tactics, but putting the cat amongst the pigeons with the trustees was the last thing she wanted to do.

"So…about that boring night of watching Sky Arts…"

Lydia looked up, seeing a warm, rather mischievous smile on Mary-Ann's face.

"Yes?"

"Wouldn't you rather go and see a film instead? There's a terrific biopic of Yehudi Menuhin on at the ICA… Oh, but I suppose you've seen it?"

"Actually, no." Lydia contemplated the evening that stretched ahead, cold and lonely in her tiny South London flat. "I'd love to."

"Fab! Let's drink up and go and see about tickets, then."

Chapter Five

The film was good, and it was just as good the second time of viewing with Milan the following afternoon. Only this time it was enhanced by the way Milan's long, pale fingers stroked Lydia's hands throughout.

He took a piece of salted popcorn and fed it into her mouth, bending to whisper in her ear.

"When this finishes, I'm taking you shopping."

"Shopping?" Lydia almost swallowed the bloated kernel whole. She hadn't figured Milan to be a man who enjoyed browsing the racks in the boutiques of the West End.

"No more fleeces," he said emphatically.

She huffed a little, but allowed him to slip an arm around her shoulders nonetheless, wondering what Mary-Ann would have to say about it if she could see their blissful intimacy. Should she have mentioned that she was seeing Milan? Oh, her personal life was nobody else's business.

She dismissed the uncomfortable thought then suppressed a squeak as Milan placed her hands in her lap and moved his own wicked fingers up to the waistband of her jeans, fiddling with the buttons until they were undone.

"Milan," she whispered, craning her neck to make sure nobody was watching them.

"Shh, it's okay. Nobody can see," he soothed, and it was true that their position in the back row protected them from curious eyes.

"But what if they *do*?" Lydia tried to clamp her thighs together, but Milan patted her upper arm in reproof, somehow winning her submission.

"They won't. Now be good, bad girl and let me have my way with you."

Lydia shuffled back on her bottom a little, spreading her legs a little wider to enable ease of access. His fingers, bunched together over her mons, crept slowly down, struggling to invade the tight space at her crotch. Looking down, Lydia saw them bulge and strain against the denim, sliding under her knicker elastic and taking possession of everything within.

She couldn't help a low hum when his fingertips widened her labia and alighted on their quarry—her fat, full clitoris, now eager and ready to accept his touch.

"Nice and quiet, Lydia," he breathed into her ear. "I'm going to make you come, but you have to keep silent."

She shook with the effort of it, gripping her thighs until her fingernails dug in while Milan circled his fingers round and round, rubbing and flicking, bringing forth gushes of juice in the process.

"Touch your breasts," he whispered, working the bud of flesh harder. "Put your hands up under your fleece and do it."

Sounds struggled to escape the back of Lydia's throat, but she bit them back and put one trembling hand inside her sweater, stroking her nipple through her cotton bra cup, finding it rock hard and almost itchy with need.

"Ohh," she whispered, anxious now that her heavier breathing could attract attention from the people in the row in front. "Please."

She threw her head back against the maroon plush and shut her eyes, tense and filled with the need to end this, to come, to regain control of her body. But Milan was enjoying his power and he teased at her needy clit, poking and prodding at the hole below for a spell, then returning to it while Lydia flicked compulsively at her nipples.

"You're so wet," he whispered. "I think you'd let me fuck you right here in the cinema. I think you'd let me put you on the stage at the front and have you right there while they all watched. What if the film was us, fucking, for all to see?"

The combination of his touch and his words did their unerring work. Lydia jolted forward and ground against his hand, gasping as quietly as her orgasm would allow, squeezing her breasts hard.

"Mmm…" He chuckled quietly, removing his hand. "You're a fast learner. I didn't think you'd let me do that."

Lydia felt at once oddly proud and ashamed. Should she have said no? Did Milan think better or worse of her for going along with his depraved plans? Was she uptight or permissive? No, she berated herself, she was simply a woman who adored a man and wanted him in every way. What was wrong with that?

"I'm not as prim and proper as you seem to think," she whispered back.

"Well, I know that after the other night. Mmm, taste?"

He put one of his fingers to her lips and she allowed him to push it in, tasting and smelling her own arousal mixed with the hot popcorn cinema aroma.

He didn't allow her to button her jeans back up until the film ended and she sat, feeling her own juices chill against her skin, her nipples still hard as pebbles, letting him knead at her denimed crotch and kiss her willing mouth until the credits rolled.

"It's a good thing I've already seen it," she remarked as they stepped out of the cinema into the brisk, bleak air of the winter Saturday afternoon. "I didn't have a clue what was going on there."

"Oh, you didn't say you saw it before," he said, taking her hand and striding purposefully towards Covent Garden. "It only came out this week. You saw it yesterday?"

"Um, yes." Lydia felt a change of subject might be in order. "So where are we going now? Are we really going shopping?"

"Yes. Who did you see it with?"

"A friend."

"A girl friend, I hope. I am terribly jealous. Strangely so, for a man who enjoys threesomes and group sex. But if you are going to fuck other men you have to have my permission."

"Yes, a girl friend," said Lydia, a mite cross and uncomfortable at having her sex life dictated to her in the middle of the street.

All the same, the irritation was ameliorated by the way every other person stopped to gawp at them, pointing and whispering.

That's Milan Kaspar from The Next Big String, she imagined them saying. *Phwoar, I fancy him rotten.*

Who's that lucky cow on his arm? Must be his girlfriend. Oh, I wish I could be her.

She held up her head and threw back her shoulders, imagining herself gliding down the red carpet with him at some glitzy televised event.

"Which girl friend? Vanessa, I suppose."

He didn't sound happy.

"No, not Vanessa."

"Good. Because she hates me and will try to get you away from me."

"Why does she hate you?"

"Never mind. Give me a name. Your friend at the cinema."

"Are you really this paranoid? You don't believe me, do you?"

"Her name, Lydia."

"Uh, Mary."

"And who is Mary? You studied with her?"

Lydia swallowed. "Mary-Ann."

Milan's fingertips pinched her arm.

"Not…the Mary-Ann I know?"

Lydia didn't answer and Milan stopped dead, swinging her around to face him while the crowds tutted and stepped around them.

"Mary-Ann McKenzie?"

Lydia made a face and looked away.

"It is! What is this? Whose side are you on?"

"I'm not on any side," pleaded Lydia. "I like her and I like you. Can't I be friends with you both?"

Milan tipped his head to one side, considering this.

"You know, perhaps you can," he said thoughtfully. His lips curved in a devilish smile and he squeezed her hands. "Perhaps that would work very well. Come on. Let's get you dressed."

He grabbed her by the upper arm and began to walk even faster than before, parting the sea of shoppers and tourists like a torpedo cutting through water.

The shop was called Maximum Vamp, and Lydia scarcely had time to admire its window display — of multicoloured feather boas and glittery scanty things — before they were through the door and inside its sartorial carnival of sex.

"This was Tilda's favourite shop," he muttered. "They know me here."

"Milan!" exclaimed a voice, as if in confirmation. A saleswoman, who looked very much like a more mature version of Liza Minnelli in *Cabaret*, emerged from the rails of velvet and satin, teeth agleam.

"Tilda? Really?" muttered Lydia, rather surprised that Milan's ex, with her polished exterior and conservative little skirt suits, had ever set foot in this place.

"Hidden depths. Like you, Lydia. Hello, Maxine, how are you?"

"Can't complain, dear man, can't complain. The season isn't our friend, of course, but we had a terrific Christmas. Now, what can I do for you? Hello."

She offered Lydia a belated nod and a smile that owed more to curiosity than genuine welcome.

"This is Lydia. She needs intensive re-styling. From the inside out."

"Hmm," said Maxine, too polite to agree but not polite enough to demur. "We can do that, of course. So you want the full service? Underwear to outerwear?"

"Yes. The full service. I trust your exquisite taste."

She simpered, then beckoned to Lydia sternly.

"We had better go into the back room. I'll send Lily out front."

They went into a room that was, if anything, even more overstuffed with sparkly fabrics than the shop. A younger woman finished her task of labelling the stock and disappeared out to the front, leaving the three of them alone to embark on Lydia's transformation.

"I'll need you to strip right off," said Maxine briskly. "Chop chop. Milan, come and have a look at the rails with me. I have some ideas, but I'll need your input."

Lydia took a deep breath. She was expected to stand naked in front of this intimidating woman? A woman, moreover, who had dressed the immaculate Tilda Fox-Boyce? She felt small and inconsequential, an inferior shop dummy, but she began to tug off her parka all the same.

"Don't worry about Maxine," said Milan over his shoulder, fingering a pile of corsets. "She has seen every beautiful woman in London out of her clothes."

But I'm not beautiful, thought Lydia woefully.

"And you *are* beautiful," said Milan, as if reading her thoughts. "You just need some help to bring it out."

She gasped, flushed and suddenly felt super-confident.

The hiking boots, woolly socks, cheap jeans and fleece were soon piled neatly on a chair, leaving Lydia shivering in sensible cotton underwear. She was very aware of the congealed essences from her cinema adventure that stained the gusset of her knickers.

Milan and Maxine emerged from the clothing jungle, laden with pieces. They exchanged a glance and smiled while Lydia hugged herself, trying to forget that she was nearly naked.

"You will be a dream to dress," exclaimed Maxine. "A lovely figure, and perfect skin." She put down the clothes and reached out a bony finger, touching Lydia's cheek. "English rose. You can carry off so many colours."

Lydia, who mainly wore brown and blue, simply raised her eyebrows.

"Thanks," she said.

"Simple white cotton suits you, but we're not about dressing down here. We're about glamming up. So take off those undies, my dear, and let's find that sex kitten inside the shy girl."

There isn't one, thought Lydia reflexively, but then she had to reconsider. What shy girl would have sex with a man while his male lover looked on, cock in hand? What shy girl would let herself be fingered to orgasm in a public cinema? She had never known this side of her existed, but it was there, and now it had seen the light it wasn't going back inside.

"I'll do it for you, if you like," offered Milan, stepping up behind her and unhooking the bra.

"Don't—" She shivered, afraid for a moment that he was going to caress her breasts in front of Maxine, but he simply took the bra off and added it to the jumble of drab clothes she had already removed.

His hands whipped her knickers down with brisk efficiency. She hugged herself, trying to cover her tendrils of pubic hair, embarrassed at the hopelessly amateur job of clipping and shaping them she had done before her date. She was going to have to investigate wax, as much as the idea dismayed her.

"I know a marvellous beautician just around the corner," said Maxine airily.

Lydia wanted to curl up and die. She stepped out of the knickers.

"Is okay," said Milan unexpectedly. "I prefer a woman to look like a woman. Is natural, there's nothing wrong with it."

Lydia turned and beamed at him, adoring him one more percentage point, bringing the total to at least three hundred and forty five per cent.

"Well, it's not the fashion, but to each their own," murmured Maxine, rummaging through a pile of the wispiest, silkiest things Lydia had ever seen. She alighted on a pair of knickers that gave the illusion of transparency, and were only visible because of the printed birds of paradise in brilliant blue and gold and the scalloped lace edging. "What do you think of these?"

She opened her mouth to speak, but it was Milan's opinion Maxine canvassed, not Lydia's.

He picked them up.

"They weigh nothing," he remarked. "I like that. She can have them."

Putting them on was like having her legs breathed on. The silk fluttered upwards and came to rest about her hips, but she could barely feel the tissue-thin fabric. It was the closest to going commando achievable with underwear and it looked so pretty, as if her own skin bore the exquisite pattern of the birds.

"Turn around," instructed Maxine, and Lydia twirled, self-conscious as she presented her bottom to the stylist and her lover, but unable to defy them.

"Lovely," said Milan.

The matching bra was of a heavier silk, the cups just crossing her nipples teasingly while the same scalloped lace covered the rest of her breasts.

"We also have a suspender," said Maxine. She clipped the gauzy silky belt on, then, once Lydia had put them on, attached it to five-denier, nude, seamed stockings.

"Walk up and down," said Milan. "Up to that mirror. Look at yourself."

Lydia saw a person she didn't recognise, with traces of herself lingering here and there. She was glad Milan had not gone for the full vamp in red or black — that was not a look she felt ready for yet, if ever. But the combination of sexy and sweet, tasteful and naughty, made her feel more feminine and fuckable than she had ever done before.

She laid her cheek against Milan's hand when he loomed up behind her and took hold of her shoulders, leaning over her to gaze at her reflection. For that moment, Maxine melted away and they were the lone lovers, enjoying their desire for one another.

"See what a difference it makes," he whispered, then he growled in her ear, causing her to shudder and visualise herself melting into a puddle on the floor. "If I could have you right here…"

He let his palms brush down her upper arms before stepping back.

"A dress," he said to Maxine. "Something to bring out the curves, yes?"

"Like this?"

She handed over a halter-necked piece in royal blue satin, polka-dotted and ruched across the chest.

Milan grinned. "Just like that."

"She'll need petticoats."

Lydia stepped into two layers of stiff netting before slipping the dress over her head. Looking again in the mirror, she was open-mouthed with awe at the sudden appearance of dangerous curves, swelling above and below her nipped-in waist.

"Every man is going to want you," said Milan. "I'll have to watch out."

"She looks fabulous," said Maxine admiringly. "She needs a strong lipstick and something doing with her hair. And some heels, of course. How could I forget the heels? Let me find some."

She returned with beautiful shoes in a Mary Jane style, but with a thickish high heel and a slender ankle strap above the T-bar, in the exact shade of blue to match the dress.

"I never wear heels," said Lydia nervously.

"You'll need to practice your walk, then," advised Maxine. "Come on. Strut. Wiggle your hips. Put one foot exactly in front of the other—it gives you a sashay."

"It's hard—I have to concentrate," said Lydia, frowning at her feet.

"Don't *look* at your feet. Shoulders back. Chin up."

Feeling as if she were performing a military drill, Lydia paced the floor until Maxine was satisfied she had acquired the skill of walking in heels.

"Perfect!" Maxine applauded at last. She tied a blue polka-dot scarf in Lydia's hair, which she flicked out to cover her shoulders. "Gorgeous. You recognised the potential there, Milan. Congratulations. But it's far too cold to go out without a coat, and that thing she was wearing before is far too offensive to the eyes. How about this?"

She held up a long black coat in some kind of matted velvet fabric, with faux-fur at the neck and cuffs. Milan shrugged and put it on Lydia, who found that it fitted quite snugly once buttoned, and was both warm and striking.

"My *goodness*, you are going to *slaughter* them out there," exclaimed Maxine. "Shall I just throw the old things away? Burn them?"

"No!" protested Lydia, but Milan was laughing at the suggestion and nodding his head.

"Keep them," he said. "If she ever wants them back, she can come and collect them."

Outside the shop, Milan put his hands either side of Lydia's nipped-in waist and gave her a long, hard look.

"Maybe I could get my hair done," said Lydia timidly, too aware of being a sex bomb only from the neck down.

"Hair done? Why?" Milan seemed lost in a world of distant thought, disconnected from reality.

"For the opera?"

"Opera? We're not going to the opera."

"Oh, but I thought—"

"The time for thinking is over. I have one thing on my mind and one thing only."

"The tickets..." But her heart wasn't in it.

"I have to take you to bed. Now."

He hooked an arm around her waist, hand tapping her hip impatiently. Then he dragged her through the Saturday shoppers and tourists, so fast she had to run, which was difficult in the unfamiliar high heels Maxine had put her in. The long velvet coat flew out behind her, net petticoats swished around her knees, and Milan bore her away to a place that now seemed ten times more appealing than the Royal Box at Covent Garden.

Chapter Six

It seemed that all the expensive wrappings and trappings had been bought only to be taken off. The moment Milan got her through the door of his flat he pushed her against the wall and began undoing buttons, his mouth all the while working on her with hungry determination. By the time the coat fell to the floor, her lips were softened and wet from kissing, her cheeks burning and legs weak. He covered her bare arms and shoulders with his hands while he nuzzled her neck. He reached around, found the fastening of the dress, worked on it with lightning speed. The petticoats went the way of the dress; then Lydia stood, or rather swayed, in her precious underwear and barely-there stockings, ready for sex. Ready to be ravished.

Milan directed his right hand to her breasts, while with his left he gripped the underside of one thigh, pulling it high to wrap around his hip. Lydia whimpered into his mouth as her pubic triangle made contact with his bulging crotch. He upped the ante, grinding it against her, maintaining the high pressure of his tongue inside her mouth.

The sensual abandonment he transmitted infected her and she lost herself in lust, twisting against him, drawing him in, glorying in the surge of blood and spirit he aroused in her. It was like a delicious, exhilarating version of a fight, a fight that would end in pleasure rather than pain. Lydia found strength she had not known she possessed, struggling to bring him closer and harder, pinching and clutching, biting and kicking, but always forced in the end to submit to his superior power.

He jammed her thighs apart, unbuckled his belt and loosened his trousers, then brought one hand beneath her bottom to lift her upward so that her feet left the floor. She whimpered in alarm, but Milan kept her pinned to the wall, firmly in position, so that she let go of her momentary panic and helped him work on getting her legs wrapped around him and her arms holding tight, ready for the act of ultimate contact.

He was able, though it didn't look easy, to reach inside a shirt pocket and find a condom while keeping her in place. Lydia hoped he was mindful of her aching spine and already straining thigh muscles and would make this fast and hard.

Once the condom was on, Milan wasted no time in sheathing himself with pinpoint accuracy, filling Lydia before she could prepare herself.

She gasped, pinned inexorably by his erection, held against the wall by his quivering body. His heart hammered, through the material of his shirt, against her flattened breasts. His eyes, when she looked up, were dark, almost angry. It felt as if he was punishing her for something. For making him want her? For what she had said about Mary-Ann? For being female, being there?

Whatever the reason, it provoked him to push strong, powerful thrusts into her, slamming her bottom into the wall, grunting into her mouth.

There was no tenderness here. All was raw and animal, barely concerned with her pleasure. She began to be afraid, began to try and push him back, but he finished almost immediately, pouring out his orgasm and accompanying it with a nip of her lip that felt as if it had drawn blood.

He drew back, gasping all over her, holding her so tightly the breath almost left her body, still inside her but softening.

"Milan," she said and her voice wobbled, on the edge of tears.

He dropped his head down to her shoulder and groaned as if in pain.

"I'm sorry, *miláčku*," he whispered. "So sorry. Did I hurt you?"

He lifted his face, searching her eyes, looking as stricken as she felt.

"A bit," she admitted, her throat still thick and tight.

"I forget, sometimes." He seemed to be speaking to himself.

Pulling out of her and discarding the condom, he gathered her into his arms and carried her into the bedroom, laying her gently on the bed while he crouched over her, stroking her sweating forehead.

"What do you forget?" asked Lydia in a broken whisper.

"That you're a girl. And girls can't always take it the same way. Evgeny likes it rough. I've got into the habit."

"I thought I was going to break." Tears slid down the side of Lydia's face. Milan kissed them away.

"I promise I won't break you. I am a stupid idiot. I get, what you say, carried away. Too much passion. I must learn to control it."

"Violence isn't passion."

"No. You are right, Lydia."

He lay down, holding her loosely, as if he thought anything tighter might snap a bone or two.

"Forgive me. I will be better next time."

Lydia let her thoughts gather like clouds as she lay in his embrace.

Evgeny likes it rough.

A plague on Evgeny and his complicating existence. Why couldn't Milan be a simple soul who stuck to one lover at a time? Why couldn't love be easy?

"I will run a bath for you," said Milan. "For the rest of the day, I treat you like a princess. No more rough stuff."

Lydia made an inarticulate sound that might have been assent or resignation, and he hopped off into the en suite bathroom and began running the taps.

She stared at her reflection in the ceiling mirror. The bite had not drawn blood, but her lower lip looked swollen and purplish. Her hair knotted and tangled all over the place and the beautiful bird of paradise on her knickers had been slashed with an irreparable rip across its plumage. Putting a hand to her inner thighs, she wondered if they would bruise — and the same thing went for her spine. Solid supporting walls were not easy on the coccyx during frantic standing-up sex, that was for sure. She would make a note of it.

The memory of Milan's brutal fucking was somehow much more potently erotic than the reality, and she began replaying it in her mind while her fingertips lingered at the crease between thigh and groin. Her clit, which had been so rudely ignored during the sex, began to awaken, sending its vibes of longing through Lydia's body, tensing it up once more after the relief of the end of the onslaught.

My turn now. She put her fingers on the swelling flesh and pressed, keeping away from the sore area below, watching herself move her other hand to her breasts, palming them slowly and rhythmically.

"Come on in—the water's lovely." She heard Milan's voice float through the en suite door. He had turned off the taps and it sounded as if he was in the bath.

"Just a moment," she said dreamily, rubbing and lifting her hips towards the reflective glass.

"What are you doing? Can't you move? Lydia?"

He sounded concerned and she clicked her tongue in exasperation, hearing him rise out of the bath and step out on to the floor. Couldn't he wait five minutes?

"Hey!" he said, catching her in the act. Dripping wet, with just a towel held in front of him, he looked mouth-wateringly gorgeous and a little bit put out. He shook a finger at her.

"No orgasms happen in here without my involvement," he scolded. "Even if I'm only watching. Take your naughty fingers out of your pussy."

"Ohhh," moaned Lydia, who had been rolling closer and closer to a sweetly anticipated climax.

"If you like, I'll put my naughty fingers in there instead," he offered, swooping down close to pull her up off her back and on to her feet. "That's quite acceptable."

"You live by some odd rules," remarked Lydia, allowing him to lead her into the bathroom, where a bath topped with extravagant foaming bubbles awaited them.

"They are my rules," he said, unhooking the bra and suspender belt. "I can't live by any others."

"Life could be hard for you, then," she said, wriggling back against him as he put a hand over her mons.

"It has been already. But no more. I live my way, no arguments. And in my life, my woman does not come without my cock, or my tongue, or my fingers inside her. You understand?"

"Your woman," snorted Lydia, but then she sighed as he found the needy clit bunched up and hidden inside the folds of her vulva.

"Mmm, this needs attention," he said into her hair. "But get into the bath first. We can do that later."

"Later!" Lydia did not think she could wait too long, but Milan's raised eyebrow persuaded her to step into the bath and defer her gratification, at least for as long as it took to get lathered up and sponged down.

Milan attended to her so tenderly that it was hard to believe this was the man who had almost fucked her through the wall less than half an hour before. Nonetheless, Lydia trusted him, and leant back against him, letting the minor aches and pains dissolve into the frothy water. She breathed in the perfume of foam washes and shampoos while he treated her body like a rare and precious gift.

"Now you're clean," he said, grabbing a bath towel from the heated rail and helping to fold her into it, "we can get you good and dirty again."

"You're insatiable," she said, hoping this might be true.

"It has been said," he admitted.

Back on the bed, Lydia lay naked and with legs spread, floating on a current of sexual magnetism and desire. Milan took his time, teasing her slowly with tongue and hands, covering every inch of her skin with thorough purpose.

He brought her to orgasm first with the tips of his fingers, then with broad strokes of his tongue. When the third wave approached, Lydia, sensitised to the point of madness, begged him to stop.

"Surely...you must want..." she panted, with a significant look at his growing cock.

"It's about what you want now," he said, bending and kissing her clit, folding his tongue over it in the process.

She shivered and tried to clamp her legs shut, but the position of his head prevented her.

"I want to make you come," she said. "Like you've done for me."

"I'd love to fuck you, *miláčku*, but I think it would hurt now..."

"No, I mean..." She tried to sit up, but he stopped her with a hand on her stomach.

"When you've come three times, we'll talk about this."

"But Milan," she wailed, her clit throbbing and unbearably ticklish.

"I want you to know what I can do to you. And this is only the start."

She lay back down. *In for a penny*, she thought. Then, *ohhhhhwoooooowarrrrrrgh.*

Afterwards, Milan let her wrap her grateful lips around his cock and suck him until he gave his essences to her, thrashing and moaning, finally in her power. Lydia adored the knowledge that she had reduced this emblem of arrogance and potency to this shivering, mewling mess just with a few flicks of her tongue. She revelled in the act, trying to spin it out until her cheek muscles surrendered and she pumped him to his final crisis.

"Do you like to give head?" Milan asked sleepily, cradling her afterwards. "Some girls don't."

"I like what it does to you. I like the power."

Milan chuckled.

"So do I. This could be interesting."

Lydia paused, not sure she wanted to mention the wilder shores of Milan's sex life in this intimate moment of coupledom, but too curious to resist.

"Does Evgeny like it too?"

"Evgeny? What about him?"

"Does he like power?"

"No, Evgeny does not like power, except as a receiver."

"And does he give good…y'know…"

"Head? Yeah. He does. Why are you so interested in Evgeny suddenly?"

"Why wouldn't I be? If you want us to work as a threesome."

"Tchah, Lydia, it's just sex. You don't have to fall in love with him. You barely have to know him."

"Do you love him?"

"Yes and no."

"Do you love anyone?"

Milan sighed.

"Not in the way you mean, probably."

Lydia looked away, then glanced up at herself in the mirror. *This will never go anywhere. I should leave.* But Milan looked so sad, so defeated. He missed having love in his life. He wanted it.

"Have you ever loved anyone?"

"It's very soon to be talking about love," he almost snapped. "It's like music, it comes when it comes. You can't force it."

"But you must *like* Evgeny? And me?"

"What, you have to like people to sleep with them? You like me? You think I'm a nice person?"

Lydia was stumped by that one. *Actually, no, not really.* But she couldn't say it out loud.

"I don't really know you," she said at last.

"No." He sounded bitterly satisfied, as if her answer vindicated his own self-loathing. "And you shouldn't want to, either. But you should want to fuck me. One thing I know how to do is fuck. And play violin."

"And conduct?"

"Yes, and conduct."

He turned his head to regard Lydia intensely.

"Like your friend," he said. "Mary-Ann."

Lydia chewed the inside of her cheek, sensing that the conversation was about to take a sinister turn.

"When did you get so friendly?" he asked.

"Last night. Bumped into her in Starbucks then went to see that film at the ICA. She's okay, Milan. I like her. She's just trying to do her job."

"It's not her job to do."

"Of course it is. The trustees appointed her."

"It should be me."

"Have you ever asked them why it isn't? Perhaps they don't know you want to conduct. Perhaps they'd be delighted to hear it."

"No, they wouldn't. They like me where I am, at the front of the violins, drawing the crowds. And besides, the trustees would never appoint me. They think I'm too...I don't know."

"Too what?" *Too Milan.*

"Unpredictable, I guess."

"Why do they think that?"

"I went missing for a couple of months once, before *The Next Big String* was made. I went to Brazil. I had to. But I didn't tell them and they weren't too happy with me."

"I don't suppose they were! Why did you disappear like that?"

"I need to get away sometimes. They forgave me because they knew I was going to be making the show and it would drive concert sales. But they don't like me. They'll never give me the conductor role."

"So why even bother with all this intrigue?"

"Because I can't do things through the proper channels, so I have to take matters into my own hands. You've seen how loyal the orchestra is to me. They want me. The public wants me. In the end, that will convince them, I'm sure."

Lydia wasn't so sure. But she was too tired to pursue the argument.

The next morning, over croissants and coffee, Milan suggested that she cultivate her friendship with Mary-Ann.

"I'm not going to be your spy!" exclaimed Lydia.

"I'm not asking you to spy." Milan came around behind her, leaning over her chair, resting his chin on her shoulder so that his irresistible warmth and clean scent flooded her senses. "I just think it would be good to know what's happening in the orchestra and she will know first. Besides, you know, she needs a friend. Since I'm such a bastard, making her life so hard." He laughed, but Lydia didn't join in. Plotting made her uncomfortable.

"I'll be a friend to her," she said, "but I'm not making any promises. Don't make me this go-between. I like a simple life."

Milan straightened. "Why the hell are you here then?" he said, a tad sulkily.

"Because I want you," she said, the words coming easily this time. "I want to be with you."

His fingers ruffled her hair. "I want you too," he said softly. "Don't think I'm going to let you get away now."

Her heart skipped, but she wished it hadn't. She wished she hadn't fallen this hard, this far, this quickly. But now it was done, and there was no way around it.

Lydia and Mary-Ann's friendship bloomed along with the snowdrops as January ice gave way to a February thaw. They settled into a routine of post-rehearsal coffees and occasional weekend dates with takeaways and DVDs, chatting long into the night about music and the frustrations of life.

Mary-Ann was certainly experiencing those.

Despite the nature of their relationship, with confidences and secrets regularly exchanged, Lydia never once let slip that she was involved with Milan as more than a colleague, although on several occasions she came very close to blurting it out.

Mary-Ann spent weeks trying every approach she could think of to get the orchestra on her side, but she seemed to be thwarted at every turn and, by the end of February, she was becoming resentful and paranoid, even beginning to doubt her skill as a conductor.

Lydia hated to hear Mary-Ann's doubts and fears, but she found herself torn. Now completely under Milan's spell, she could find no way of helping her friend that would not compromise his position. Sometimes she lay awake at night, thinking that he really deserved to have his mean-spirited little scheme exposed...but then he would reach for her, pull her close, murmur in his sleep. She would wonder what nightmare shadows were passing through his mind, what caused that expression of infinite sadness she saw behind his devilishly glinting eyes.

Despite her best intentions and the dictates of her head, she knew she had fallen in love. The stupid urge to fix him, to make him whole and happy, consumed her.

You can't change him, she chided herself. Then her good sense would be undone by a little voice saying *probably...*

Floundering in these dangerous waters, she fell deeper into Milan's vortex, knowing she was being groomed for her place in the threesome, but wanting to carry on, to find out what would happen, how it would work, *if* it would work.

To this end, she found herself, one blustery Saturday in early March, waiting in the restaurant of an art gallery for Evgeny to meet her for lunch.

Over the preceding month, Milan had divided his time between her and Evgeny, never pushing the ménage concept when she didn't seem ready, though he occasionally speculated on things they could do in bed, to quite devastating and orgasmic effect at times.

Staring at the menu, Lydia thought of the previous night's sex, her on all fours while Milan held her shoulders, all the better to pound into her.

"Next time you're in this position," Milan had rasped from behind, "perhaps you'll have Evgeny's cock in your mouth. Or maybe you'll be riding Evgeny while I fuck your arse."

Lydia had groaned and clenched her fists around the sheet. They hadn't tried anal sex yet, but Milan had been preparing her — with well-lubricated fingers and a selection of toys—over the course of the week, so she knew it was on the cards soon.

"Would you like that, Lydia?" His words travelled over the rough slap-slap-slap of their connected bodies. "Would you like to be fucked by two men at once, using you hard, giving you what you need?"

Yes. But I don't want to admit it. But yes.

"Are you okay?"

Lydia dropped the menu, aware of the heat in her cheeks, and looked up at Evgeny. She hoped he didn't have the ability to read minds. Although, perhaps that would make this whole deal easier. Some things were just too hard to talk about.

"Yeah, fine," she said. "Tube's gone to shit again, hasn't it?"

Evgeny sat down, grinning that sparkly-clean grin.

"Engineering works everywhere," he agreed. "What's good to eat here?"

"I was just going to have a club sandwich and coffee."

"Okay, but I've just come from the gym. I need more than a sandwich. Maybe some pasta."

They spent an awkward, artificial ten minutes discussing the finer points of the menu, studiously avoiding any conversation that did more than skate on the surface of the situation.

Only after the food arrived, when Evgeny had speared a pasta shell, chewed on it and swallowed, did he deliver the words they had both been putting off.

"Milan wants me to fuck you."

Lydia's bite of club sandwich turned huge and indigestible on her tongue. She struggled to get it down, then nodded.

"I know. He thinks we should get to know each other in and out of the bedroom. How do you feel about it?"

Evgeny raised his eyebrows, looking down at his pasta.

"It's fine," he said. "You're a nice girl. You know, I'd maybe ask you out if I wasn't with Milan, anyway. So…"

He shrugged.

"Do you…are you in love with Milan?"

"Of course."

"Do you ever wish you could be exclusive?"

Evgeny sneered.

"I suppose you do?"

"I'm asking you."

Evgeny sniffed and leant back in his chair.

"I like to play the field," he said. "Milan allows me to do that. As long as I tell him who I'm fucking, he'll let me do what I want."

"So it suits you — this arrangement?"

"Sure it suits me. I get lots of sex, and some of it's with Milan, who I love. It's good."

"I suppose so."

"You sound doubtful. I know your type. I've seen this before. You want him for yourself. Well, it won't ever happen. He won't be tied down to one person. He won't even be tied down to one gender, so why don't you give up on that little idea and share the wealth?"

"You've seen this before?"

"So many times. Boy, it's boring. Like your friend Vanessa. She couldn't handle it, wanted Milan all to herself. Greedy bitch. He dropped her like a stone. So get your head together, Lydia. Accept that, if you want him, you have to share him, or get out."

"Don't you ever get jealous?"

There was a beat of silence before Evgeny said, "No."

He's lying.

"So, are we going to have sex?" said Lydia.

"That's the plan."

"Even though you obviously don't like me?"

"What's that got to do with it?"

Lydia thought back to Milan's words. She didn't have to like Evgeny. She barely even had to know him. How odd it all was.

"A lot, surely! Isn't it a bit weird to have sex with someone you don't like?"

"No. I do it all the time. It's kind of good. Different, but good."

"You can cut the sex part of yourself off from the feelings part?"

"Easily. Can't you?"

"Umm..."

"So you *like* Milan?" Evgeny laughed incredulously. "He's a bastard. Come on. You have to agree."

"He might be a bastard, but I love him. That makes the sex...that's what the sex is *about*."

Evgeny's lip curled in disdain. "Love," he said. "It's such a stupid thing."

"I know that. But we both love him, don't we? And that's why we're doing it, when it comes down to it. It's got nothing to do with sex—it's all about love. Your love, and my love, for Milan."

Evgeny's lips turned down.

"Think what you like," he said, hunching his shoulders. "I'm doing it because I fancy a shag and you're here."

"Well, that's certainly not why *I'm* doing it."

"I know. But you have to try sex with a person you don't like. Let me show you how it can be."

Lydia pushed her plate away. "This is weird," she muttered. "Even by recent standards."

"What's weird? You fancy me, don't you?"

She looked him over, long and thoughtfully. He was very attractive, beautiful really, with a look of Rudolph Valentino about him. Not many girls would pass him up, she supposed. If only he didn't have the pouty, prima-donna personality to match.

"You're pretty," she said. "Pretty on the outside."

"You don't know me. You don't know anything about me."

"You're from Minsk and you play the cello and you're Milan's lover. And you don't like me."

"And that makes me ugly on the inside?"

"It makes you unappealing to me. It's only natural."

She flinched as Evgeny's foot brushed her ankle under the table.

"No, that's not natural. I can show you what's natural."

"Evgeny…"

He moved his foot up her calf, rucking the denim, prodding little dints in the heavy fabric.

"Don't you want what Milan wants? What I want?" he said softly, caressing the back of her knee with booted toes. "Don't you want to have us both? All our attention on you and what you want? Wouldn't you like to have four hands touching you and two tongues licking you? I know you would. I know what you are. I know you dream of getting fucked by two horny men at once. Don't you, Lydia?"

Blood roared in Lydia's ears. Her jeans were uncomfortable, hot around the crotch. Evgeny found her thigh and moved his foot inexorably upwards.

"Answer me, or I'll get under the table and get those jeans off you right here."

Lydia's throat was dry, but she managed to croak, "Let's go."

Evgeny beamed and gave her crotch a nudge of approval before withdrawing his foot.

"Milan's out but he said we could use the flat. As long as we promised to film it all."

"Film it?"

"Just for us. He likes to watch."

Evgeny threw some money down on the table and drew Lydia away by the elbow.

For you, Milan, she thought, clattering down the gallery stairs behind the Belarusian. *I hope you appreciate this.*

Chapter Seven

Budapest, Hungary
One month later

From the hotel window, Lydia could look out across the Danube to the castle on the Buda side of the city. She took in its ancient winding paths and turrets before turning to Vanessa, her roommate, and sighing with appreciation of the beauty around her.

"What a place," she said.

"The Paris of the East," remarked Vanessa, unpacking toiletries from her suitcase and ranging them on her bedside table. "Or so they used to say."

"How many times have you been here?"

"This is my third, I think," said Vanessa, wrinkling her brow. "These tours all become a bit of a blur after a while." Her expression softened and she smiled at the younger woman. "But you never forget your first. We've got a whole day to ourselves before rehearsals start tomorrow. Why don't you get your coat and I'll show you some of the sights?"

Lydia bit her lip, looking away.

"I promised Milan…"

Vanessa sighed heavily, thumping a can of deodorant down on the table.

"Oh, of course you did. Milan."

"I know you don't approve—"

"Damn right I don't."

"But he's good to me, Ness. He's never done anything to hurt me. We're happy."

"Secretly happy. Don't you ever ask yourself why you can't make your relationship public? He isn't committed to it, Lyd. Don't kid yourself he ever will be."

"Perhaps I just want sex," said Lydia belligerently. "Perhaps I'm not necessarily looking for happy ever after."

"Just as well, because you won't get it, not from him."

Just because you *didn't*, thought Lydia rebelliously, but she didn't say the words. She liked Vanessa, despite her pursed lips on the matter of Milan, and valued her opinion.

"I must admit," she said, looking back out to the cityscape, "I wish he'd drop all this crap with Mary-Ann. She doesn't deserve it. Sometimes I physically itch to write to the trustees."

"Why don't you?"

"I can't be the one to rock the boat. I'm the newbie here. Why don't *you* tell them?"

"If I grass Milan up my life won't be worth living. But he likes you—seems to even care about you. Perhaps he'd forgive you, if you spilled the beans. Made it look like an accident, or a drunken confidence…"

"Don't, Ness. I can't do it. Don't make me feel bad."

Vanessa shrugged. "He seems to have eased off her a bit lately, anyway."

It was true. Rehearsals over the month of March had been relatively pleasant with only occasional spanners thrown into the works by her jealously intense lover. She had a feeling, though, that he might be saving up his big guns for this tour.

He had been good-humoured for weeks, spending lots of time with her, devoting his attention to their developing relationship. While he encouraged her to sleep with Evgeny, he never pushed her into anything, taking time to ease her into the triad dynamic. She was even starting to quite like the cellist and understand what made him tick. At bottom, he and she had a lot in common. Their mutual love for Milan was only a part of it.

But tonight was to be the night. The first proper threesome.

Lydia shivered a little, then was galvanised into action, remembering that she had arranged to meet her two men in the lobby in five minutes.

"Let's hope this tour goes smoothly," she said, reaching for her jacket to ward off the April blusters. "Where do you recommend we visit, then?"

Vanessa lay down on the bed, lacing her fingers behind her head.

"Oh, Milan'll know everywhere," she said. "You don't need me."

"Yes, I do," said Lydia. "Don't say that."

Vanessa smiled ruefully.

"Okay," she said. "You don't need me...yet."

Vanessa was right—Milan knew everywhere, and he took them to all the best and most beautiful places, finishing off at the elegant Café Gerbeau where he bought them fresh cream pastries and hot chocolate.

As soon as the last crumb was eaten and the last blob of cream wiped from the tip of her nose, Lydia felt the mood shift. The day of innocent pleasures was about to morph into the night of guilty ones.

Evgeny seemed to tense, his eyes flicking rapidly between Milan and Lydia. Milan braced an arm on the backrest of his chair, letting his head recline against his hand, the pose too deliberately relaxed to actually be so. The playfulness in his expression swept away, replaced by serious shadows. He looked at Evgeny, then Lydia, for a long time.

"That was nice," he said at last, as a waitress cleared the plates and cups and left their bill. "But there was a lot of sugar. I like sweet things sometimes. Sometimes I don't."

"Don't talk in riddles," begged Lydia.

He laughed.

"Okay. You are nervous, yes? You want to do this?"

She glanced over at Evgeny, whose face was open and relaxed. It reassured her, and she nodded.

"You are free to walk away any time," said Milan quietly. The waitress took the coins, avoiding their eyes. She seemed to understand that the three customers were experiencing a *moment*.

"I know that," whispered Lydia. "I don't want to walk away from you."

Milan ran a hand through his hair, holding the fingers close to the scalp for a contemplative second or two before withdrawing them with a flourish and a tumble of locks — a gesture that never failed to quicken Lydia's pulse.

He offered his fingers to Lydia, reaching out to her across the table.

"Let's do this, then," he said.

Lydia walked back to the hotel arm in arm with Milan and Evgeny, meeting the curious eyes of passers-by with a lascivious smile. *Yes, both of these gorgeous men are mine. Aren't you jealous of me?*

Milan, alone of all the orchestral players, had his own hotel room, and a double at that. He invited Lydia and Evgeny to sit down on the bed while he retrieved a laptop from one of his travelling bags and began fussing with it.

"What are you doing?" Lydia asked, wondering anxiously if she should be touching Evgeny or getting naked straightaway. How did these things get started?

"I thought we could get in the mood with a little video. One of my favourites. You and Evgeny, that first time."

"Oh, I've never seen it!"

"I know. Why don't you pour us all a drink from the mini-bar, hey? Champagne might be appropriate."

Lydia, grateful for the nerve-calming alcohol, poured the fizz into two wine glasses and a tooth mug, which were the only receptacles available. She took the tooth mug for herself and tipped back a mouthful of bubbles while Milan placed the laptop on the bed in front of her and took his position at her rear, leaning over her shoulder while he clicked to open the relevant file.

At first, only a brownish gloom showed on screen, but then there was a gusty sound and Evgeny appeared in shot, looking spectrally pale, his dark eyes burning coals. He leant forward, adjusting something, and the colour contrast improved dramatically. He took an elaborate bow to the camera, then reached forward, directing it towards the bed in Milan's Barbican flat.

Lydia breathed in sharply, seeing herself sitting on the edge of the bed, looking apprehensive.

Milan put an arm around her stomach, hugging her back against him.

"You look so scared, *miláčku*," he crooned, kissing her hair.

"I was," she whispered.

On the film, Evgeny's voice rang out from just outside shot.

"Are you wet yet?"

Lydia-on-film looked disgusted and clicked her tongue. "Is that how you seduce people, Evgeny? Porn dialogue?"

"Oh, oh, oh, excuse me!" Evgeny swooped into shot, pulling Lydia to her feet and dancing lightfootedly around the floor with her. "Is that what you want? Seduction?"

She laughed as he whirled her around, a high, giddy sound.

"Evgeny!"

Out of breath and pink-faced, they span to a halt, then Evgeny bent to take a kiss and the camera caught their mouths crashing together and their tongues battling forward, while Evgeny's hands explored the length and breadth of Lydia's body.

In the hotel room, Lydia began to feel her body drift out of her control, her nipples stiffening and her pussy melting in anticipation of those hands on her again, plus two more.

Milan, attuned to her racing pulse and flushing cheek, unbuttoned her shirt and slid his hand inside, his lips dabbing at her neck and shoulders.

"Put your hand on her leg," he told Evgeny, who obeyed, clapping his palm on her stocking-clad knee and rubbing it, tickling the sensitive skin underneath.

On the film, the kissing couple had tumbled backwards on to the bed and were rolling around, limbs entwined, hair everywhere.

Evgeny had managed to straddle her, ruthlessly divesting her of her striped, long-sleeved T-shirt, then her jeans. In socks and underwear, she wriggled beneath him in a pretence of reluctance, but he leant forward and pinned her by her upper arms, diving back into a kiss that ended much farther down her body than it started.

Her bra was next to go, leaving her breasts vulnerable to the voracious hands and teeth of the Belarusian, who took full advantage of them. While Evgeny-on-film nipped and lapped, Evgeny-in-reality inched Lydia's skirt upwards. The nylon of the stockings felt humid and clingy now, and her knickers were soaked. Milan was unabashedly fondling her breasts inside their bra cups, whispering in her ear about what a filthy, fuckable little slut she was and how she was going to get the seeing-to of her life that night. Lydia moaned as Evgeny reached her stocking top and his fingers hit bare thigh.

On the film, Lydia was naked. Evgeny had unbuckled his belt with a matador flourish and flung it across the room. He growled and pushed Lydia's legs wide apart, then began to eat her out with the single-minded determination of a wild animal while she uttered broken sounds and hid her face from the camera with a forearm.

"How did that feel?" Milan's voice was silk in her ears, taking her mind off the pinching in her nipples. "Evgeny's tongue on your clit?"

"He was rough and greedy." She sighed. Evgeny's fingers were inside her knickers now, dabbling in the juices they found there. "Like a ravenous wolf."

Both men chuckled at the image.

"Looks like he's getting a feast," said Milan. He eased Lydia's shirt off and unhooked her bra, then reached down for the zipper of her skirt. Evgeny took over, shifting it down over her thighs while Milan bit and sucked at the base of Lydia's neck, ravaging the soft skin there.

Once Lydia was down to hold-up stockings and knickers, Evgeny returned his hand to the wetness beneath the silky material, but this time his fingers were joined by another set.

Lydia lifted her bottom from the bed and moaned as the two men fingered her ruthlessly, covering every part of her slick, sensitive sex while she ground against them. The film blurred and distorted, though she vaguely knew that, in it, Evgeny was fucking her now, his taut muscled arse rising and falling with gathering speed while the camera watched indifferently.

In reality, the champagne glasses lay abandoned on the floor while Lydia lay back and spread herself, at the mercy of her two lovers, one of whom — she didn't know which — wrenched down her knickers and pulled her thighs wider. She arched her knees and stared at the whirling ceiling, wishing it was mirrored like Milan's so she could gaze up at the decadent tableau they must make.

Fingers were everywhere, between her lips, flicking at her clit, pushing up inside her cunt, stroking her skin and pulling her bum cheeks apart. One of them had a hand on her breasts, kneading and pinching them while the hard work went on below.

"We're going to make you come and come, and come again tonight," said Milan, and his words came out in savage puffs of warmth on her clit, his hair brushing her thighs. "You're going to lose count."

She heard herself cry out in orgasmic rapture on the laptop, and her real voice joined the recorded version while she bucked and kicked against the force of her climax, spending on two sets of hands, feeling two sets of male breath laugh against her pussy.

"You're definitely ready," said Milan. "We've trained you well. Okay." He switched off the video recording. "Now to the real business. Come down, *miláčku*, come down, that's right." He stroked her hair and kissed her forehead until her breathing regulated.

Evgeny kept a steadying hand on her thigh, as if he thought she might rear up, though nothing could be further from her mind.

"Was that good?" whispered Milan. "From the way you are trembling, I think it was."

"Good," said Lydia faintly. "Very."

"Well, Evgeny, I think we are wearing too many clothes. Let's let Lydia catch her breath for a minute while I..."

Lydia watched Milan reach over to the other man and pull him forwards by the belt of his trousers, which he proceeded to unbuckle. Lydia hadn't seen this look on Evgeny's face since that fateful, rainy night at the Barbican when she had first become aware of their relationship – he seemed to transmute from sulky, arrogant brat to adoring submissive at the first hint of Milan's touch. His wide, lash-fringed eyes betrayed a vulnerability Lydia had rarely seen and he lifted his arms, wordlessly allowing Milan to pull his sweater over his head and expose his pale, hairless chest with its peaked little nipples. Milan pressed a fingernail into one of the nipples and Evgeny gasped, tensed slightly, but didn't withdraw an inch.

Next, the trousers and boxers came down simultaneously, and Evgeny's erect cock sprang up, only to be firmly enfolded in Milan's fist and given a brief pump.

"It's not just Lydia who's ready," commented Milan. "You're always ready, aren't you, slutboy?"

"Yes," breathed Evgeny, his eyes closed and head thrown back. "God, yes."

"Have you seen this, Lydia?"

She certainly had, and she nodded to that effect.

"Of course you've seen it. Lots of times," Milan continued. "You've had it in your mouth, your pussy, between your tits. Where do you want it now?"

"Mouth," said Lydia, who had decided beforehand that Milan would be the man to fuck her properly, while Evgeny could pick up what was left.

The Belarusian did not look disappointed with this deal, however, and he smiled wickedly as Lydia rose to her knees and took his shaft in reverent hands. She glanced up at him before bending her head to her task—he looked like a czar, proudly ruling over his concubine. So different to the way he had looked for Milan. Lydia felt a moment of misgiving, wondering if she was making the biggest mistake of her life, but then Milan gave a gentle nudge to the nape of her neck and she plunged down, accepting the familiar, bulbous end of Evgeny's cock into her mouth.

Her tongue worked deftly while her lips stretched, letting him in inch by inch. Behind her, she registered the rustling of clothes, then the snap of rubber. Milan had a plan.

"He tastes good, doesn't he, *miláčku*?" The seductive voice was close to her and he placed a hand on her flank, stroking it up and down. "I know he does. I make him eat half a pineapple every day, you know. It sweetens the juices."

Lydia almost snorted mid-suck, but she held her nerve and carried on.

"Your juices don't need sweetening, do they? Let me check."

She whimpered, despite her full mouth, as Milan dipped a finger between her pussy lips and ran it back and forth until it was coated. The smacking sound of his lips and a long, 'Mmm...' expressed his verdict.

"No, quite sweet enough," he said.

Then his hands were on her hips and his chin and nose nudging inside her thighs, and he pushed his tongue up inside her, gorging himself while she quivered under his attentions. Evgeny put a hand on top of her head, holding her in position as if he were afraid she might pop off and abandon him in favour of Milan's masterful tongue. She sucked harder, not wanting to disappoint him.

Milan drew a final zigzag around her clit then took his mouth away, keeping his hold on her hips and positioning her so that her bottom was raised and her thighs wide.

She had to stop sucking at the moment of penetration, needing to revel in it without distraction. She always loved that instant of being entered, filled and taken, especially by Milan whose cock was the perfect satisfying length and width. Slackening her lips around Evgeny's manhood, she waited until Milan's haunches bumped hers before resuming the blowjob with a vengeance.

She was tossed back and forth like a ship on a rough sea, pushed forward by Milan with each thrust so that Evgeny had to shift a little bit farther back until his feet hit the headboard. Then they achieved an ideal state of tension, with Evgeny resisting Milan's efforts to force him into the wall, so that Lydia felt she was being crushed from both ends, caught between the rock of Milan and the hard place of Evgeny.

Suddenly her mouth filled with saline creaminess and Evgeny yanked at her hair while he puffed and sighed above her. He managed to hold her tight while Milan continued to fuck her, caressing her breasts all the while. Lydia kept her mouth over Evgeny's softening cock, somehow needing it to feel complete, while Milan moved closer and closer to her G-spot.

"Look at her, Evgeny. She can't stop sucking you."

"I know. She likes to have her mouth full."

"Did she do it right?"

"Oh yes. She's had practice."

"I know Lydia never misses a practice..." Milan panted, and Lydia flew into her orgasm, gripping Evgeny's thighs hard and moaning around his cock. This seemed to give the signal for Milan to let go of himself and pour out his own climax. The room seemed to spin and surge with sex as the three of them collapsed into a steamy embrace, kissing and sighing into inertia.

The evening had only just begun.

It continued with room service, spoon-feeding, cream smeared on breasts and licked from fleshy crevices, bubble baths full of slippery limbs, more champagne, Milan and Evgeny showing Lydia how the boys do it, Milan and Lydia showing Evgeny how to do it standing up, more kissing, more tongues, more fingers, more orgasms.

When midnight struck, Lydia and Evgeny were in the sixty-nine position while Milan slid a lubricated finger up Lydia's back passage, testing her for resistance.

"This is what comes next," Milan told her darkly, rotating his fingertip inside the tight little space, finding the limits. "I want to have your arse while Evgeny takes your cunt. I want to have you filled so full you can't think. I'm going to do the dirtiest things you can imagine to you, and I'm going to make you want them."

Lydia came, for the fifth time that night, almost weeping with exhaustion, over Evgeny's tongue. Milan's finger in her bottom made her feel so bad, so used, so filthy and so hot. She had a vague feeling she ought to be ashamed of herself, and that turned her on even more.

Evgeny conceded defeat. "I don't have any more in me," he said, letting Lydia off the hook — or the cock. "I give up."

Milan released Lydia from his anal explorations, and she sank back into his arms, yawning.

Evgeny stood up, dishevelled and slightly flustered.

"You want to shower?" Milan asked lazily.

"Yes. But I'll do it in my room."

"What? You aren't staying the night? Hey, the bed is big enough."

"It's okay. I want a bit of space now."

Lydia felt the muscles of Milan's forearm stiffen around her stomach.

"What's this bullshit? Space? You've never wanted to leave early before."

"I need my sleep, Milan. It's too uncomfortable with three in the bed. It's okay. I'm fine. I'll see you at breakfast."

"Hey!"

But Evgeny leaned over and silenced him with a lingering kiss before throwing a towel around his middle, picking up his clothes and leaving.

Lydia twisted round to look up at the perplexed face of her lover.

"Do you think he's really okay with this? With me?"

Milan kissed the tip of her nose.

"I thought so. He hasn't said otherwise. He likes you, he says so."

"I don't think he does. Not really. I think he's jealous of me."

"Lydia, Lydia." Milan moved so that they both lay flat on the bed, wrapped around each other. "Who could be jealous of a sweet thing like you? Especially one that gives such great blowjobs?"

She kneed him gently in the thigh and pouted.

"Life's not all about sensual gratification, you know. There are things called emotions too."

"Is that right? Nobody told me."

"God, you're such a jerk sometimes. I really wish I didn't want you so much."

"Unlucky for you. Lucky for me."

"But seriously, Milan…if you had to choose between us…"

"It won't come to that. Shh, now. We should sleep."

He threw the duvet over them and burrowed down beneath it, kissing away her fears and her misgivings, at least for that night.

Waking up with Milan in a king-size bed in Budapest was one of the shining moments of Lydia's life. Tired and aching as she was, she breathed in his smell of man and sex and faded aftershave and her clit tingled despite herself. This man had turned her from a demure violinist to a raging sex maniac, she reflected ruefully. But there was no way around it. She wanted him all the time, every waking moment.

Watching his face in sleep, she bent over and kissed his ear, then his cheek, then, when he didn't wake up, his neck and shoulder. She gave in to the temptation to nibble at his firm, pale flesh, wanting to bite into that succulent swan neck, but before she had the chance he woke and rolled her over, pinning her down.

"It's never enough for you, is it?" he said hoarsely, rubbing his morning erection between her pussy lips. "Aren't you sore and worn out from last night?"

"Yes," admitted Lydia. "But there must be things we can do..."

There were things they could do. Mindful of her raw pussy and puffy clit, Milan eased himself gently into her wet slit and took her for a slow, leisurely ride. Lydia still felt the pain, but she embraced it, opening herself to his tender attentions and soon forgetting the sting as the pleasure built. He rocked over her in tiny movements, keeping her mouth filled with his tongue, bathing them both in sensation.

When the wave crashed over Lydia, she found herself saying, "I love you, I love you, I love you." Luckily the words weren't coherent, falling as they did into Milan's throat, so he never heard them.

What if he had? Would it have mattered? Would it destroy everything, or would it lead somewhere new? Lydia didn't dare rock the boat—it was unsteady enough already.

Instead, she joined Milan in the shower, dressed and went down to breakfast.

Evgeny was already at the buffet, helping himself to fruit salad and yogurt.

"Are you okay?"

"Of course." He turned to her, watching her fill her bowl with cereal, stony-faced.

"Where are you sitting? Can I join you?"

"Aren't you going to sit with Milan?"

"He wants to get an hour's practice in first. He'll be down later."

They took their dishes to a corner table and waited in guarded silence while a waitress poured their coffee and took requests for hot dishes.

"Why did you leave last night?" Lydia opened, once she was sure they wouldn't be overheard.

Evgeny's lips curled sulkily.

"I told you. I sleep better in my own bed."

"That's why you spend so many nights at Milan's place, is it?"

"That's different. It's late. The tubes aren't running. It makes sense to stay. Here I have a bed of my own, paid for. Why not use it?"

"Evgeny, if you think I'm taking Milan away from you—"

"I don't. I don't think that. I don't think you could, anyway. You aren't enough for him."

"What do you mean?"

The cereal felt dusty and lumpy in her throat. She swallowed it with some effort.

Evgeny drew a breath, as if gearing up for a lengthy expulsion of bile. Lydia flinched in advance.

"There is no substance to you," said Evgeny. "You have no history and you've never suffered."

"I… What?"

"There are girls like you in orchestras all over the world. Young, bright, optimistic, naïve. Milan collects them like china ornaments. I don't know how many he's had. He keeps them until they start to lose their optimism and their naïveté, then he gets bored and loses interest. Sure, he's taken a shine to you for now, but it won't last."

The cereal plunged, leaden, to the pit of her stomach. Lydia felt horribly breathless, Evgeny's words like a punch in the solar plexus.

"That's...an awful thing to say," she wheezed. "You make him sound like—"

"I make him sound like what he is. If you can't handle it, get lost." Evgeny shrugged and bit into a strawberry.

"And what's so special about you? If you don't mind me asking." Lydia fought to keep the tremor from her voice, temporarily winning the struggle.

Evgeny smiled.

"I know him better than you ever will. I know his land and I know its past. I know how it feels when your talent is the thing you depend upon to get you out of hell."

"Hell? I thought Prague was supposed to be quite nice." Lydia couldn't resist a sarcastic laugh.

Evgeny banged his spoon on the table.

"You know nothing! You've lived your comfortable life with your bourgeois parents, enjoying every privilege the West can give you. You know *nothing*."

Evgeny's face had whitened with fury. He pushed his bowl aside and stalked off, leaving the coffee half drunk and Lydia's mind bursting with questions.

She deliberately dawdled over her breakfast, wanting to speak to Milan about the encounter, so by the time he appeared in the room she was chewing slowly on her third piece of toast, draining the dregs of her fourth coffee. At least she might stand some chance of staying awake for rehearsals, she thought. Plus, all last night's action had left her with an enormous hunger, so the extra breakfast wasn't unwelcome.

"Milan," she said urgently, drawing him over to her table with his cup of coffee and croissant. "Evgeny is being weird with me."

He sat down, rolling his eyes a little. "Weird? How?"

"I think he wants me to finish things with you."

"No, he doesn't."

"He does! He said—"

"Lydia!" Milan's tone was sharp and his lips thinned into a straight line. "I'm not a teacher for you to tell tales. I get enough of that from Evgeny."

"So Evgeny tries to turn you against me?"

Milan sighed. "Perhaps this is all too much. Perhaps I need to take a break from it all."

"You want to break it off?"

"Well?" He opened tired-looking eyes again, raising his eyebrows. "If you and Evgeny are going to squabble all the time, it'll drain too much creative energy. I can't have that. Neither can you. None of us can afford that level of distraction."

"But I…that's not what I want."

"It's not what I want either. Good. So you and Evgeny will play nicely, yes?"

"If he will, I will."

"He will. I'll make sure of it."

"Are you going to talk to him?"

"Maybe. Lydia, I thought we were happy. I thought everything was good."

"It is! Honestly. This is the time of my life—look, here in Budapest, playing in a world class orchestra…and you. Having you in my life. I couldn't ask for more."

Milan smiled, a little weakly. "Neither could I, *miláčku*. Neither could I."

"He said…he said you'd been through hell."

Milan shook his head. "Typical Evgeny. So dramatic."

"What did he mean?"

"Nothing. Come on. We have a rehearsal. Go and get your violin."

Chapter Eight

Mary-Ann tapped the music stand with her baton.

"Right then, guys," she said. Lydia noticed how her style had altered over the weeks, from humorously ingratiating to unsmiling and brisk. Even in three months, the woman had aged visibly. "We have two days of rehearsals to get this absolutely down. The concert is tomorrow night, and it has to be good. A lot is riding on this. So I'm banking on your own professionalism and pride in your skills to get us through it. You are the talent — I'm just facilitating that talent."

Milan grunted softly, but Lydia could tell that the speech pleased him. Mary-Ann had been underplaying her contribution to the performance more and more every week, until she'd begun to paint herself as some kind of passive vehicle, barely relevant to the music at all. She had lost confidence. Surely she wouldn't last much longer.

"We have two Hungarian Rhapsodies, a set of Hungarian Dances and the Kodály Háry János suite to get through. I think we might as well start with a quick Hungarian Dance—number one, first things first."

Lydia, caught up in the music and transported to the Hungarian plain where the wheat waved and the orchards hung heavy with ripening fruit, didn't notice at first that the tempo was slipping. But when the moment came to pick up the original speed, it was a horrible mess, half of the violins coming in at least a beat behind the others.

Lydia looked sideways at Milan, noticing his cheekbones twitching mischievously. She pursed her lips, annoyed with him for orchestrating this new rebellion, and moved her gaze to Mary-Ann, who was shaking her head vigorously and tapping the music stand.

"Guys, guys! We've done this perfectly before. What happened there? Milan?"

"You're the conductor—you tell me."

"You're the orchestra—haven't you heard of watching the conductor? Following her beat?" Mary-Ann's voice had risen to an unprecedented level and was shaking—she really seemed to be on the verge of losing her temper in grand style.

"Maybe you should let the *ritardando* come to its natural conclusion before picking up the beat?" suggested Milan, in such a sardonic tone that half the violinists snorted.

"Oh, really? That's what you would do, is it?"

"Yes, that's what I would do. I think you pick it up too quickly."

"Oh, and do you know what I think? I think *I'm* the conductor and *you* play the thing the way *I* say."

"The last note in that phrase is far too short. Who agrees?"

A forest of hands shot up to endorse Milan's statement. Lydia half-raised hers, then put it down again, seeing the shimmer of tears in Mary-Ann's eyes.

"Milan," she whispered, but he was too busy enjoying his moment of triumph.

"I don't care what you think," stormed Mary-Ann, waving her baton around rather wildly, jabbing it to emphasise her point. "You've made it obvious that I'm not welcome, and if I conducted it that way you'd say that was wrong too. So just shut the fuck up with your constant undermining and do what you're told."

Milan put down his violin and folded his arms. A third of the string section followed suit.

"There's no need to swear at us," he said softly.

A tear of frustration spilled from Mary-Ann's eye. Flinging down her baton, she turned and fled the rehearsal room.

"Oh, well done, Milan," said Lydia sarcastically, though her words were drowned by the uproar that had broken out. Laughter and backslapping gave way a couple of minutes later to earnest discussion as it dawned on the orchestra that they had a concert the next day, and no conductor.

"I don't want her, but she can't quit right now," said Milan thoughtfully. "Lydia—she likes you. Go after her. Talk her around. Promise her we'll play Budapest the way she wants. Don't make any promises for Prague, though."

"Milan, just lay off her! I feel awful for her."

"Your tender heart," said Milan, ruffling her hair infuriatingly. "Hey, I could just step in and save the show. But that would ruin her career, don't you see? So if you go and persuade her to come back, you are doing what's best for everyone."

Lydia sighed, grabbed her bag and headed out of the hall, figuring that the women's restroom was as good a place as any to start looking.

But Mary-Ann was not to be found there, so Lydia left the building and scanned the street beyond. On a park bench in a small garden to the side of the concert hall, the routed conductor sat with her face in a handkerchief.

Lydia dashed down the steps, calling her name.

"Go 'way, please," said Mary-Ann, but Lydia took a seat beside her.

"Hey," she said awkwardly. "Don't be upset."

Mary-Ann sniffed and laughed without mirth.

"How does that work, then? Everybody works together to trash my career and I'm supposed to be happy about it?"

"Not everybody."

Mary-Ann turned pink-rimmed eyes to Lydia and grimaced in concession.

"No. You're right. Some of you aren't in league with the devil himself."

"The devil himself?"

"Milan." She laughed hollowly. "I wonder where he hides his horns and his forked tail."

"Oh, he..." Lydia quelled her impulse to defend him. What he was doing was indefensible. "He wants what you've got," she said instead. "He's jealous of you. That's all."

"I don't understand it," said Mary-Ann. "He's famous, a brilliant musician, everyone seems to think he's some kind of sex god. Why the hell would he be jealous of me?"

"He wants to be in charge. He hates being told what to do."

Mary-Ann put her handkerchief back in her jacket pocket and frowned at Lydia.

"You've made quite a study of him."

"No, not really. It's common knowledge. In the orchestra, anyway."

"So tell me. What else should I know? About Milan, and the WSO in general?"

"Oh, I'm no expert. I'm the rookie."

"I know that. It means you haven't been sucked in yet. You see things with a clearer, more objective eye. Perhaps you can help me, Lydia."

"Do you really think so? Why don't you come back up? We need you, you know."

Mary-Ann exhaled her dismissal of this idea.

"Nah. I'm done with backbiting violinists for the day. Tell you what. Why don't we go and get some lunch and let them get on with it. Maybe I'll come back tomorrow for the concert, maybe I won't..."

"Well, okay," agreed Lydia, seeing a spark of hope present itself. "Where shall we go?"

"Have you been to Margaret Island?"

"Not yet."

"What are we waiting for, then?"

Lydia emerged from the ladies', having texted Milan a message about what was going on. Now she was free to relax and chill out in the company of a person she liked and respected. Milan could do his worst, but she wasn't going to join in with the sabotage of Mary-Ann's conductorship.

Margaret Island was a beautiful green oasis in the middle of the Danube, boasting its own thermal spa resort, and it was in the cafe of this healing environment that Mary-Ann and Lydia chose to escape the hurly-burly of orchestral life.

"What am I going to do, Lydia?" asked Mary-Ann, pouring the first of many glasses of wine.

"Come back and conduct the concert," said Lydia, more confidently than she felt. "It's not just the reputation of the orchestra at stake — it's your reputation too. Don't ruin that for the sake of some silly spat with Milan."

"It's a nightmare, though, Lyd. I've never experienced anything like this. Don't you find the atmosphere awful to work in?"

"Well, I'll admit, it's not what I was expecting."

"What would happen, do you think, if I complained to the trustees about Milan?"

The wine glass tilted in Lydia's hand, almost slopping rich Hungarian red over the rim. "Oh, don't do that," she said quickly.

"Why not?"

"Because most of the orchestra, and pretty much all of the strings, would go with him if he left. And he would leave. And the trustees don't want that. He's a money-spinner, now he's done all that media-darling stuff."

Mary-Ann contemplated this. "Yes, I do see that. So what's the solution? I leave and let him take over?"

"Stick it out for this tour, at least," said Lydia. "I don't think he'll mess up the concert. His own pride wouldn't let him do that."

"You're right. Good. Okay, let's finish this bottle, then how about a boat trip on the Danube?"

Much later, after a trip on a boat and a walk up to the Fisherman's Bastion, Lydia and Mary-Ann found themselves in a bar near the hotel, still avoiding the rest of the orchestra, continuing a long and rambling conversation about their childhoods, families, musical influences and adolescent crises.

"God, it was painful," lamented Mary-Ann over yet another glass of Bull's Blood, her spectacles now a little crooked over her nose. "I literally thought I was the only lesbian at my school and nobody else ever, ever had those kinds of feelings about other girls. I couldn't tell anyone. Then I got friendly with a tuba player at youth orchestra—Joanne, her name was—and thought perhaps she might understand. She tweaked my underdeveloped gaydar—cropped hair, lumberjack shirt and so on. But my gaydar was rubbish. I came out to her and she just laughed and told the rest of the brass section, who kind of avoided me after that."

"That's awful! Why were they so mean?"

"Oh, you know what kids are like." Mary-Ann seemed to intend the comment to be throwaway, but Lydia saw the telltale dazzle of tears at the corner of her eye. She put one of her hands over the conductor's and squeezed it.

"Not just kids," she whispered.

A teardrop fell onto Mary-Ann's cheek. She rubbed it away angrily. "Oh God, Lydia, ignore me. I've just had too much to drink and it always makes me sentimental and self-pitying."

"No, that must have been devastating. I know how sensitive I was when I was fifteen."

"Well, that wasn't so long ago, was it?" said Mary-Ann softly. "Listen, Lydia...I might be way off-beam here...and I did tell you my gaydar was dodgy...but..."

She leant forward. A sudden surge of enormous panic sobered Lydia within seconds.

"Oh, look, we're both a bit squiffy, Mary-Ann. Might not be the time for anything that can't be taken back."

Mary-Ann halted, a little waveringly, and narrowed her unfocused eyes.

"God, yeah," she slurred. "Not the time...not the place...sorry. Just want some company... So lonely in my hotel room..."

"I'll keep you company," offered Lydia, her brain instantly screaming, *What are you thinking?* "Just for tonight. If you like. If you promise to come back to rehearsal tomorrow."

"Of course. Was going to anyway. Right then." Mary-Ann fumbled in her jacket pocket for money and dropped a fountain of forints ostentatiously on to a beer mat. "Lesh go."

Lydia had to help Mary-Ann get undressed – the Bull's Blood seemed to have overtaken her own blood in her veins, and she was barely able to stand by the time they had barrelled into the hotel room.

By the time she laid her on the bed in her pyjamas, Mary-Ann's eyes were shut. She began to snore gently a few moments later.

Lydia tried to text Milan, but her fingers were clumsy and the words didn't come out right. Eventually, after several attempts, she managed to get 'Am with Mary-Ann, she is ok, c u 2moro xxx,' on to the screen without too many typos. Her work for the day done, she fell onto the bed next to Mary-Ann and plunged into a fully-clothed sleep.

"So, how are you today?"

"Shh, not so loud." Lydia winced as Milan slid into the seat beside her at the breakfast table.

He laughed. "Did she get you drunk and take advantage of you?"

"No, she didn't. Well, not the taking advantage part anyway. And she's in a worse way than I am this morning. She's gone for room service. I suspect the rehearsal will be pretty short today."

"Are you sure there was no girl-on-girl action?"

"Don't sound so disappointed."

"You can tell me. I won't judge."

"Shut up, Milan. The main thing is, she's going to conduct tonight. In the meantime, have you got any Advil?"

Despite Mary-Ann's feverish eyes and ghostly pallor, the Budapest concert was a triumph, and standing ovations were their reward for all the aggravation and difficulty of the past months. As she rushed past Milan and Lydia, clutching a vast bouquet, she muttered, "Thanks."

Milan laughed, watching her scurry backstage on the way to the Green Room.

"Thanks, she says," he remarked. "She doesn't have a clue. Wait till we get to Prague."

Vienna came first, though, and as the tour bus bowled through the Hungarian countryside and over the border to Austria, the sun came out, promising more than Lydia thought the visit might deliver.

She sat next to Mary-Ann on the coach, listening to her hyper-excited chatter about a series of Mahler centenary concerts, but when they arrived in the heart of the old baroque city she disengaged from the conductor and sought out Milan.

"I have a treat for you tonight," he said, inviting her into his room.

Evgeny was already there, fresh from the shower in a towel and nothing else.

"Really?" asked Lydia, envisaging a grand banquet in some archducal palace, or perhaps a night at the opera.

"I've just had a call from my old friend Werner. He's put us on the VIP list for his club tonight."

"Club? I didn't think you were into clubbing."

Lydia's imagination turned to some strobe-lit cattle market for gilded Euro-princelings, where a bottle of water would set you back a small fortune and shady-looking DJs spun Lady Gaga discs all night long.

"Not that kind of club," said Milan obliquely. "It's very exclusive. Let me help you dress."

To Lydia's surprise, Milan produced from his case a tiny scrap of golden fabric, shimmery and thin, and put it on the bed.

"What's that?"

"It's your outfit. I brought it with me, just in case Werner was in town."

"I don't understand. You packed clothes...for me?"

Milan nodded impatiently while Evgeny lay back on the bed, chortling.

"What's this club, Milan? What's it about?"

"It's a sex club."

"A sex club? You want me to go to some club to have sex? Jesus, Milan!"

"No, it's not like that. I thought you might like to watch the show, that's all. If you don't want to join in, that's up to you. Evgeny and I probably will, though."

"What is it? Like burlesque? Strippers?"

"No, nothing like that. Just like-minded people who enjoy performing. Exhibitionists, you could say. And voyeurs. I think you know me well enough to decide which one of those I am."

Lydia's mouth flapped open and shut.

"Come, Lydia. Nobody will make you do anything you don't want to. It's on a voluntary basis. If you just want to watch, that's okay. If you don't want to watch, you can leave."

"I…" Lydia looked again at the tiny scrap of fabric on the bed.

Evgeny sat up, grinning.

"And the food is amazing," he said. "It's an old palace from the days of the Hapsburg Empire. You feel like old-fashioned royalty when you're there. Old-fashioned, decadent royalty."

"Do you?" Lydia's curiosity began nibbling at the edges of her reserve. This sounded less like the pit of sleaze Milan had painted.

"Absolutely," said Evgeny. "It's not some backstreet brothel. You might even find somebody famous at the table with you."

"More famous than me?" Milan pouted, then grinned devilishly.

"Well…okay," said Lydia. "It sounds interesting, at least. But do I have to wear that?"

"Well, you can't wear a fleece, *miláčku*. Not to take supper with the Crown Prince of Mauretania."

"Okay, okay, but I could wear my concert gown."

"That thing? Drab black sack. No. This is what you wear if you go."

Milan's word was final.

Lydia shrugged and picked up the dress. It would skim the very tops of her thighs and the neckline plunged as low as was decently possible.

"You can't wear anything underneath," said Milan helpfully.

"What? Not even a thong?"

"Nothing. Just that and a pair of heels."

Lydia, feeling a little like a lamb being prepared for the slaughterhouse, allowed Evgeny and Milan to lead her into the shower.

They washed, lathered and perfumed her, lotioned her naked body, then rubbed it all over with golden sparkly gel that made her skin gleam in the light.

Evgeny treated her breasts, while Milan helped the unguent sink into her buttocks, working them thoroughly with a cupped palm.

"Do I really need a golden bum for this?" she asked aloud.

"Oh yes," Milan purred into her ear. "For us, if no one else."

Breathless and aroused by her lovers' attentions, Lydia tried to draw their attention to the wetness between her legs, parting her thighs a little and pressing them into Evgeny's groin.

He laughed and patted her hip.

"Later, darling. We must all wait our turn."

She was short of breath and flushed beneath the gold flecks by the time Milan wrestled her into the dress. If you could call it a dress. A scanty sheath of almost-sheer gold stretch material, it outlined every single curve and left her erect nipples plainly visible. The plunging neckline reached almost to her navel — a hand would only have to brush against her lightly to draw the fabric aside and expose a breast. The flirty, flippy skirt rustled just beneath the swell of her arse cheeks — the most minimal pivot of the pelvis would lift it up and reveal all.

"You look like a whore," said Evgeny admiringly.

"I know," said Lydia, dubious at her reflection in the mirror.

"You look like *our* whore," expanded Milan. "Which is how we want you to look."

In the mirror, Lydia watched as Milan stepped up behind her and clasped her around the waist, his long, white hands crossed over her belly, fingertips resting lightly at the top of her pubic triangle. *Move lower*, she silently implored, but he simply rested his chin on her bare shoulder and turned to kiss her neck.

"What do you think, Evgeny? Too fresh-faced. We need to plaster on some makeup."

By the time they were ready to leave the hotel room, Lydia had lips dripping with scarlet gloss, eyelids of gold and eyelashes blacker and thicker than midnight. Her feet were strapped into golden stilettos with four-inch heels, on which she tottered unsteadily, still unused to anything without a thick, grippy sole. She had to rely on Milan's and Evgeny's arms to support her as they travelled down in the lift and out through the lobby. Thankfully, her long velvet coat concealed her shockingly explicit attire, but all the same, passers-by would likely mistake her for a prostitute.

In the taxi on the way out of town, Milan and Evgeny pointed out every tourist attraction they passed, despite the darkness that had fallen over the city. Eventually, though, the buildings grew sparser, the road wider. They were heading into the woods, somewhere hidden and remote.

Chapter Nine

The car turned down a bumpy track road, under canopies of branches, winding and twisting through the pitch-black forest until they arrived at a set of huge gates.

Milan took out his phone and punched in a brief message.

The gates opened, slowly and mechanically, and Lydia looked along a driveway of half a mile or more to where a handsome rectangular Schloss stood at the far end. Its tall, thin windows burned with golden light and she could see vague shapes flitting inside.

"It really is a palace," breathed Lydia.

"What did we tell you?" said Evgeny smugly. "Werner is one of the richest men in Austria."

Milan and Evgeny helped Lydia from the cab and up the steps, where a splendidly uniformed man waited by the giant front door.

In German he asked for their names, which Milan was happy to give in the same language. Then they were led inside to a place of chandeliers and cherubs, pillars and porticoes, pink plaster and golden ornamentation.

At the entrance to a busy drawing room, the guests were announced.

Every eye fell on their trio. Lydia calculated that that made about fifty eyes in total, for there were between twenty and thirty other guests. Most of the men, like Milan and Evgeny, wore formal evening dress, though one young man sported only leather shorts and a leash around his neck.

The room glowed a glamorous gold, and its female occupants seemed to carry the theme over to their outfits, most of them in some form of metallic, shiny garb. Lydia surmised that there must have been a dress code that Milan had not seen fit to explain.

Drawing closer, she was shocked to recognise a pair of very famous, married movie stars and she dropped her eyes, fearing that she might not be able to stop staring if she didn't. As for the rest of the people in the room, they represented varying ages and nationalities, but most were attractive and all were groomed to perfection. She felt a very poor specimen beside the modelesque women in their diaphanous column dresses, but Milan squeezed her hand at exactly the right moment and she tried to dismiss her insecurities. She was here with one of the most famous violinists in the world.

A man with a red sash across his dress shirt strode forward, arm extended.

"Milan! So good to see you again." His accent was distinctive but not thick, and he wore small-framed, wire-rimmed glasses over his large nose. "Though I keep reading about you in the international press. Your stock is rising, it seems."

"Werner." Milan and his friend exchanged brief embraces with back slaps. "You remember my friend, Evgeny?"

"Ah, we all remember him. It's a pity our friend the gymnast couldn't be here tonight. He was very taken with your Evgeny the last time you visited. And who is this charming young person?"

Lydia blushed and looked at her gold-shod feet as Werner's sharp eyes rested upon her.

"This is Lydia, one of our violinists at the WSO. She's an open and curious girl. She wanted to see what happens at your parties. I'm hoping she'll find it to her taste."

"So am I, so am I." Werner held out a hand, which Lydia shook shyly, a little disappointed that Milan hadn't introduced her as something more than a work colleague. "Welcome, Lydia."

All eyes in the room watched as she accepted a flute of champagne along with her escorts. They drew her into the midst of the crowd, Milan making confident small talk with everyone while she and Evgeny eyed each other. He seemed almost as overwhelmed by it all as she did, she thought. Did he feel like some kind of gilded accessory for Milan, the way she did?

As she nodded acknowledgement to the beautiful female movie star, a horrible thought occurred to her. Milan had said it was fine to just watch. But what if he wanted to join in? Could she really sit there and watch him make love to that Hollywood goddess over there? And, if he could have her, surely he would not want a meek, middle-of-the-road mouse like Lydia any more?

"Hey," he whispered, turning suddenly to her after a baffling conversation with a famous flamenco dancer about some mutual friend of theirs, "are you okay? You're very quiet."

"I've never been anywhere like this before," confessed Lydia. "And I can't get over the Linberghs being here! I mean, he was voted the world's sexiest man last year, wasn't he? And I'm in a room with him."

"Oh, don't be starstruck, *miláčku*. He's a pompous bore. And she's a spiteful diva. You're worth ten of them." As an afterthought he added, "They are good in bed, though."

She felt a little more confident then, pushing back her shoulders and lifting her neck. So many eyes were upon her, sizing her up, drinking her in. She had never been looked at this way — so boldly, so blatantly — before. It gave her a sense of power. She was wanted and desired, and she could take or leave the wanters and desirers. No wonder people were so concerned with their appearance, if this feeling was the result of looking good. She had never understood it before, but now she began to see the appeal.

"I just need to speak to Sir Anthony."

Milan's fingers left her elbow and she felt abandoned, cast adrift on a spangled sea. She hid in her champagne glass, drinking too quickly, but then Evgeny offered unexpected refuge, materialising beside her and putting a hand on her shoulder.

"The first time is a head trip," he said. "I remember."

"Have you been here many times before?"

"Only once."

"What happens, Evgeny? What will happen later?"

"There will be dinner, conversation, then…entertainment."

"What's the entertainment? Sex?"

"Yes."

"Did you…do it?"

"I watched. Last time. I think I'll have to take part tonight."

"Have to? Don't you want to?"

"Yeah, yeah, sure I do. Of course."

Lydia wasn't convinced, but she had no chance to pursue the conversation as a gong sounded, indicating that dinner was ready.

She was relieved to find herself placed beside Milan, but Werner sat on her other side and she had the feeling he would pride himself on being an attentive host.

She wasn't wrong.

"How long have you and Milan been friends?" he asked. *Friends?*

"Since I joined the orchestra – in January."

"Not long. What do you think of my little place here?"

"Little place? It's vast! And very beautiful."

"Thank you. I like it. So many things have happened here, Lydia, you wouldn't believe it if I told you. Every single act man and woman, or man and man, or woman and woman, or multiples thereof, can possibly do together. It's all happened here. Do you have experience of parties like these?"

"Er, not really."

"Oh, that's good. So we can teach you a few things. We do love fresh blood."

The female movie star, Natasha Linbergh, chimed in.

"Just as long as the old guard get their fun too."

"Darling Natasha, you know you've never left my premises unsatisfied."

She laughed throatily. "I guess that's true. Milan, do you remember that time with the sex swing in the garden?"

Lydia tried not to pinch her lips, but it was hard. Something gave her the impression that Ms Linbergh was playing footsie under the table with Milan as well. She moved her foot sideways a little and hit a flexing calf. Bitch!

Milan, gratifyingly, moved his legs back and tucked them under his chair.

Ms Linbergh pouted and shot a daggers glare at Lydia before discussing her latest waxing with the man on her left.

The food, Lydia assumed, was exquisite, but somehow she couldn't bring herself to swallow more than a couple of forkfuls.

"So, Milan, will you and your guests be performing for us tonight?" Werner asked.

Lydia stiffened.

"We haven't decided yet," he said, putting a hand on her thigh. "We'll see what the evening brings."

The evening brought a move into a large drawing room behind the banqueting hall, and the guests seated themselves on luxurious chaises longues and divans while fruit and petits fours were passed around with the postprandial liqueurs.

"Who will be first?" asked Werner from a throne-like seat in the corner of the room. "Who has prepared something for us?"

Lydia sat on a cushion at Milan and Evgeny's feet, leaning back against Milan's shins while he stroked her hair.

She twisted her neck to grin knowingly at him when the Linberghs were first to volunteer. Who would have guessed?

She relaxed her muscles and prepared for a show. The Linberghs, stunning and sexy, wouldn't be hard to watch, at any rate.

To applause, they strode into the centre of the room, where a velvet- and silk-covered divan, piled high with cushions, awaited them.

Mr Linbergh — Ross — took Natasha in his arms and they swooned into a passionate kiss, just like so many of their movie clinches, perfectly photogenic and calculated to arouse.

On breaking the embrace, Ross turned to the audience and spoke.

"You know how much Natasha and I love to get down and dirty for you, and we've been looking forward to tonight ever since we both wrapped up our latest projects. But tonight we want to add a little something to the show."

Lydia's heart started racing. Why were they looking at Milan?

"Tash has never forgotten the time she and Milan gave the triple-O performance some of you might remember."

Some enthusiastic nodding and muttering broke the fascinated silence.

"So I'd like Milan to join us," Natasha said, beckoning a finger. "If that's okay with you, honey?"

Lydia held her breath.

"You're putting me on the spot," demurred Milan. "Lydia?"

Lydia had no idea what to say. She knew she didn't want to watch Milan fucking Natasha, but, on the other hand, she didn't want to be the one responsible for dampening the party spirit.

Ross seemed to pick up on the reason for the hesitation.

"If you want young Lydia to join in, that's cool. Lydia, I'd be honoured."

His gleaming movie star smile beamed right at her. Ross Linbergh, the Oscar-winner, was inviting her to take part in a foursome. Every woman in the place stared at her with jealous expectancy, along with several of the men.

"If you don't want to, it's okay," whispered Milan.

"But then you—"

"I don't need to fuck Tash Linbergh. I've done it before. We can sit this out, it's fine."

But Ross Linbergh's piercing blue eyes and his tousled beach-blond hair were just feet away, his vibrations of desire radiating towards her, the vibes joined by the almost tangible waves of Natasha's need for Milan. When would a chance like this come again?

"I'm not scared," said Lydia, half to herself, half to the room. "I can do this."

"I'm very proud of you," murmured Milan, hiding his words in the gale of applause that greeted their rising to their feet.

Lydia was lightheaded as she crossed the rug to where the golden couple awaited them. Natasha was first to seize her and crush her against her bosom, which felt surgically enhanced inside its Grecian column dress. The scent of priceless crushed flower petals emanating from the movie star dizzied Lydia, who accepted a voluptuous kiss on the lips while the room's approval buzzed in her ears. Then she was handed over to Ross, who turned her out to face the room, clasping strong arms around her until his fingers found the hem of her tiny dress. Once they'd curled inside, he began to flip it teasingly up and down while his lips dug into the soft flesh of her neck.

She could see Milan grabbing a fistful of Natasha's hair and tilting her head back for a fierce kiss. It looked so hot she almost forgot Ross's manipulations and the eyes of the audience on her, until she noticed Evgeny's face.

Thunder.

Oh, dear.

She shut her eyes then, willing the sight out of her brain so she could concentrate on letting her nerves dissolve into the sizzling steam of sensuality. Ross brought her around so that her face was pressed into his shoulder, then tipped her chin up to claim a kiss. A movie star kiss, she thought, trying to deconstruct it for signs that it came from no mere mortal. But it was simply a good, workmanlike kiss. It didn't set off any of the stars or fireworks Milan could charm out of her, but it was perhaps more like one of Evgeny's kisses — urgent and hard and a bit over-eager.

His big hands rested on her bottom, pulling at the skirt until Lydia knew that the lower portion of her cheeks must be visible to all. He squeezed them with those movie star hands and delved between her thighs, making her stand with them slightly parted.

"Very nice," she heard someone in the room say. "A sweet little pussy made to be fucked, there."

"Nice bum too," remarked a woman. "No cellulite, lucky bitch."

With his other hand, Ross pulled aside one of the flimsy triangles of chest-covering fabric, so that one breast with its rosy nipple, tight and stiff, popped out and brushed against his suit jacket.

When Ross freed her mouth, she couldn't help but dart a glance over to Milan, who had Natasha on the bed already, hovering over her and covering the exposed parts of her with flicks of his tongue.

"Hey, a guy could feel hurt," teased Ross. "You've really got it bad for Milan, haven't you?"

"He's the one," she whispered.

"But I can make you feel good too, sweet thing. Let's get that dress off you and show you how."

Somebody had put some music on, something primal with a low, thumping bass line. The rhythm worked on Lydia like hypnotism and she followed its lead, swaying as she held up her arms so that Ross could slip the tiny dress over her head.

She felt fingers dancing down the hollow of her back and she shivered against Ross's body, craving a firmer touch, which he was happy to give. She ground her hips against him to the music, rubbing against the fabric of his expensive dress trousers.

Milan and Natasha had both stripped naked and were kissing passionately on the divan, their long, lean limbs sensuously entangled. The way his hair hung down over Natasha's face sent a stab of intense jealousy to the centre of Lydia's being. This was how he must look when he was kissing her. Why wasn't he kissing her now?

"Okay, okay." Ross sighed. "Let's go and ask if we can play too."

"I'm sorry," Lydia whispered.

"It's your first time. You're hung up on this guy." Ross kissed Lydia's cheek, took her hand and sat her down on the edge of the divan, inches from Milan's and Natasha's flexing feet.

He took a few minutes to undress, making sure that Lydia enjoyed the full effect of his honed physique and mastery of movement. Oh, yes, he was stunningly good-looking—of that there was no doubt. His skin was a sun-kissed gold and every muscle stood out in clear definition. His chest, when he eased out of the crisp white shirt, was a work of art and the stomach below was flat and hard as steel.

Then her eye was unavoidably drawn to what lay beneath the jaw-dropping abdominals and she had to stare. It was pierced. Two ends of a silver crescent curved from the glans of Ross' cock, each tipped with a rounded ball. Didn't that *hurt*?

She only realised that her mouth was hanging open when Ross crouched in front of her, laughing softly.

"Take a closer look," he invited. "What do you think of my Prince Albert?"

"That must have *killed*," she breathed.

"No, not really. One of the best things I ever did. Really adds a lot to the sensation. For me and my partners. Go on—touch it."

Lydia hardly dared put out her hand, but she brought a fingertip to the adornment and pushed at it, half-fearing that it might cause Ross to scream in agony. But he simply made a murmur of encouragement and jutted his hips forward. She handled his cock as if it were made entirely of precious metals rather than pierced flesh—delicately and with care.

"It's okay, honey. It won't break."

She wrapped a fist around it and tugged.

"Oh, yeah," said Ross, with a shudder.

An animal sound from Natasha distracted Lydia into turning her head and dropping her new toy. Milan was laving her breasts, the nipples dark berry-red and shiny from tonguing. She saw his hand, the hand she watched every day wielding a violin bow, moving subtly between her legs, knuckles rippling as the fingers probed.

I want that, she thought. *I know what he's making her feel. I know the way he uses his fingers.*

"Yes, watch them," murmured Ross, turning her to face them and leaning behind her with his hands on her shoulders. "Watch your lover with his fingers inside my wife. Doesn't she look amazing like that?"

"Flawless."

But Lydia took little pleasure from the sight.

Milan lifted his head from Natasha's breasts and shot a glance at Lydia.

"You like this too, don't you?" he said. "Ross, bring her around where I can see her and have her sit on Tash's face while you play with her from behind."

The beat of the music drummed in Lydia's ears and she kept her mind on it, the slow pound, pound, pound, as Natasha forced her tongue way up inside Lydia and Ross caressed her breasts and stomach. His piercing rubbed and pushed between the cheeks of her arse until she worried that he might go too far and breach her virgin opening. And throughout this double battery of lust, she had to watch Milan feasting on the woman who feasted upon her.

He was like some beautiful sinewy beast, in absolute control of his own body and Natasha's, knowing exactly how to move, where to target, how much to give and how much to hold in reserve. The look of ferocious concentration on his face was so like the way he looked when in the throes of making music — Lydia comforted herself with the idea that he viewed Natasha as no more than another form of violin, an instrument to be played and mastered.

Natasha came under his hand and Lydia felt the other woman's tongue flap wildly between her pussy lips, the breathing coming hard and fast, steaming her up inside.

"Oh yes," crooned Ross into her ear from behind, nudging his cock further and further inside her cheeks. "Is that turning you on, baby?"

Lydia began bucking into Natasha's mouth, vaguely hoping that she might suffocate the movie star. Milan was looking at her now, watching her keenly as if she were a contestant on that stupid TV show he'd done. Was he going to mark her performance — success or fail?

"Milan," she said, reaching out to him, impervious to the joint efforts of Natasha and Ross. They might as well be on the other side of the room as far as she was concerned. "Please."

"I'm sorry," said Milan, apparently to Ross. "She's a little greedy for my attention. Perhaps if I..."

"Oh, sure," said Ross, lifting her off Natasha's face. "How do you want to do this?"

"Lydia," said Milan, taking her hands and pulling her into a tight embrace. "Let me make a suggestion. Ross is feeling left out, and that isn't fair, is it?"

She shook her head against Milan's chest.

"Come down, *miláčku*, down."

His hand exerted gentle pressure on her shoulder until she was kneeling opposite him. He took his cock in his hand and pumped it a few times, then put a hand beneath Lydia's chin, running a thumb along her lips to part them.

"You know what I want, *miláčku*?"

She nodded, happy to be given this chance to connect with Milan. She sensed Natasha's eyes on her, lazily scornful, but she determined to look only at the man she loved and nobody else.

With her eyes fixed on his face, she opened her mouth and bobbed forward, first darting out her tongue to flick the underside of his glans, then sealing the tip with her lips. A tremble of Milan's hips signalled his deep pleasure and she began to suck, reaching out to encircle the base of his cock with a finger and thumb, the way he'd taught her. She tried to keep her gaze up at him, hard as it was on her neck, clearing her mind of the audience and the other players in their foursome, concentrating on her work and his satisfaction.

Noises to their left indicated that Ross and Natasha were fucking enthusiastically while they watched. *I guess they don't do this because they're bored with each other*, Lydia thought. She flicked a look over to them, then couldn't tear her eyes away, entranced by the two beautiful bodies in erotic combination.

"He's hot, isn't he?" panted Milan to her, pushing her head down further as she sucked. "You could have him. Don't you want him?"

Ross and Natasha were bound up in some elaborate contortion from the later pages of the Kama Sutra. Lydia wasn't sure she could even hold that position for longer than three seconds and she watched in awe as the pair demonstrated the elasticity of yoga gurus. The look on Ross' face as he slid in and out of his wife's pussy was electrifying and arousing—so much passion and determination written across his handsome brow. Lydia began to think that perhaps she'd been hasty in dismissing the prospect of fucking him.

Natasha came as the music reached a thunderous climax, her manicured oval nails digging into Ross' firm backside.

"Ross," urged Milan. "Take Lydia. Take her while she sucks me. That's okay, Lydia, yes?"

Lydia could only nod, feeling the edges of her reality mist over with steam and lust. She spread her thighs and pushed out her bottom, ready for Ross' hard prick, anticipating its size and feel.

His hands grabbed her hips and his cock glided in.

"I won't last long," he warned.

"That's okay," said Milan, the words coming with an effort now.

Ross began to thrust and Lydia felt herself pushed forward, Milan's cock jerking farther down her throat. Caught between two cocks, she tumbled into a dark well of sensation, finding a pleasure in her submission that she had never before experienced. Her cunt widened, opened up by a stranger's cock, though it was hard to think of a man she had seen so many times on film as a stranger. At the same time, she sucked harder, needing Milan's spunk in her mouth, her reward for a job well done.

She got it, plenty of it, shooting to the back of her mouth while Milan pulled at her hair and heaved out a sigh. She swallowed the cream and let Milan lift her head and kiss her, long and hotly, through her own orgasm and, finally, Ross'.

"Nice," said Natasha sardonically. "I guess you aren't such a good girl as you think."

Lydia, her face hidden in Milan's chest, made no reply, but her body froze in anticipation of further hostilities. The applause of the audience drowned her words, but they were sharp enough for each of the foursome to catch.

"Did you think you were better than me? Is that why you wouldn't fuck Ross at first? You're no better than me, sweetie. You'll take cock from anyone. Tell you what, Ross, let's invite her round. I'd love to go to town on her with my strap-on."

"Okay, Tash, leave her alone," said Milan. "You were confident your first time?"

Ross laughed.

"Are you kidding? She walked out before anything happened."

Tash huffed and stalked out of the room, clutching her clothes.

Milan clung to Lydia, stroking her hair and kissing her head.

"You were so brave," he whispered. "You were brilliant. I love you."

She emerged from her refuge to stare up at him.

"Do you?"

"Of course. You know I do."

Did she? But before she could pursue the thought, Milan had rolled her over on to her back on the divan, covering her body with kisses, and Ross had joined in.

Kissed and licked into perfect relaxation, she lay there, naked and dreamy, watching Ross and Milan make out, then make love, through a haze of satisfied longing.

She didn't notice Natasha return to the room until she pulled Ross out from underneath Milan and barked, "We're leaving."

Lydia sat up and watched Natasha snatch Ross' clothes and hurl them across the floor. With one hand covering his recently vacated arsehole, Ross hopped around the room, swearing and plucking at the scattered garments before chasing Natasha out into the lobby.

"Oh, dear," said Lydia.

Milan's face reflected his irritation at being interrupted mid-stroke and his cock pointed rebelliously towards the departing figure of Ross.

"Fucking divas," raged Milan, which struck Lydia as a little ironic.

He removed the condom and discarded it then, reaching for a fresh one, appealed to Evgeny.

"Evgeny, help me out here."

But Evgeny simply stood and walked out after the movie stars.

"I think the party's over," said Lydia.

Werner stood and begged his guests not to be put off by this small setback, asking if anybody else wanted to perform.

A gaggle of enthusiastic libertines rose from their seats. It appeared to be Lydia's cue to get dressed.

She pulled the scrap of gold fabric over her head, relishing the prospect of getting a shower and a good night's sleep, but Milan, dishevelled and devilish in his crumpled black tie suit had other ideas.

Taking her hand, he led her over to a sofa and sat her down.

"Aren't you going after Evgeny?" she asked tentatively.

"No. If he wants to sulk, he can sulk. I'm not going to ruin Werner's evening by running out on him. I want to get another invitation some time. Unfortunately, I don't think Evgeny's name will be on it."

"Will mine?"

Milan gave her lips a lingering kiss.

"Oh yes. You will be more than welcome, I'm sure."

She sat, half asleep, through the whipping of the man with the leather shorts and a variety of additional humiliations. There followed a more general orgy, from which Milan released her by paying his respects to the host and leaving, pleading early rehearsals.

As they passed through the lobby — Lydia yawning hugely and carrying the gold stilettos, no longer caring about going barefoot — she caught sight of a shadow behind a bust of some nineteenth-century archduke.

"Oh, Evgeny!" she said.

He emerged from behind the plinth, scowling, tie loosened and collar undone.

"You are still here," said Milan coldly.

"I have no money for a taxi," he replied.

"You have legs."

"Milan, come on —" pleaded Evgeny.

"No, you come on. There's no room for jealousy in my cab. I'll see you."

He pulled Lydia along beside him, out of the door.

"Milan, it's miles — you can't leave him here."

"He didn't have to come. He didn't have to leave. I don't have to take him home."

The cab was waiting for them in the driveway. Milan nudged Lydia on to the back seat, from which she saw Evgeny running down the steps, shouting.

"Would you do that to me? Leave me somewhere with no way of getting back?"

Milan, sliding into the seat beside her, tutted and tossed his hair, but didn't reply.

"Because that's not the kind of man I want to be with, Milan. That's not the kind of man I like at all."

Milan tutted again and put a hand on the driver's shoulder, instructing him to wait.

"Okay," he muttered, winding down the window. "Get in, then. But if you're going to sulk, you can get straight out again."

Evgeny threw himself into the front passenger seat and clicked his seatbelt.

"No need to thank me," sniped Milan. "Though it isn't me you've got to thank. I'd have left you there. It's Lydia."

Evgeny twisted his head around to glare at her.

"Thanks," he said, though the word sounded like an insult.

"Don't mention it," said Lydia.

The journey passed in silence.

Chapter Ten

The Viennese rehearsals and concerts went well enough for Mary-Ann to regain a modicum of her confidence. At breakfast on the morning of their departure, she breezed through the buffet over to the cereal station, alighting on Lydia, who had to look away from trying to work out whether Milan and Evgeny were making up over pastries and coffee and try to appear interested in company.

"Good morning, lovely one," trilled Mary-Ann, filling a bowl with muesli. "Ready for part three of our odyssey?"

"I think so," said Lydia, busying herself with the toaster. "I'm sitting over there with Vanessa, if you want to join us."

"Thanks. Last night went brilliantly, didn't it?"

"Fantastic. They loved your *Tales from the Vienna Woods*."

"Did you think so? I thought so."

They made their way to the table, joining Vanessa.

"I believe the Czechs love music every bit as much as the Austrians," said Mary-Ann optimistically. "We should have a full house for tomorrow's concert."

"Let's hope our resident Czech is in a good mood," remarked Vanessa pointedly. They all looked over at Milan, who wasn't looking as full of the joys of spring as Mary-Ann.

Lydia inhaled sharply as Evgeny kicked back his chair and stormed out of the breakfast room.

"What is it with those two?" wondered Mary-Ann. "They seem to have a volatile relationship. I didn't think Milan was gay."

"He's bisexual," said Vanessa, her tone flat.

"Really?" Mary-Ann was all ears, leaning forward and speaking in a loud whisper. "So he and Evgeny...?"

"On and off," said Vanessa. "Milan's a busy man, if you know what I mean."

"You don't seem to like him much."

"That's because I used to like him a bit *too* much."

"Oh, God, really? I don't want to pry..."

"It's okay. I'm over it. I was infatuated for a while, and he's very good at playing on that kind of adoration. Until it gets too serious—then he gets bored and moves on. It's just Milan. As long as you don't want anything from him, you can have a good time with him."

Lydia buttered her toast over and over, not daring to catch Vanessa's eye. She didn't want Mary-Ann knowing about her relationship with Milan, not now. Somehow she didn't feel she could bear the other woman's disappointment.

"A bit of a playboy, then?"

"Kinda. Isn't he, Lyd?"

Lydia looked up sharply and shook her head, shrugging at the same time.

"I guess. He's dated lots of semi-famous women, hasn't he?"

"You know he has."

"I don't really care about that." Lydia felt moved to defend him, although she risked exposure by Vanessa. "He's been good to me. As the leader of the orchestra, I mean."

Vanessa snorted.

"He encourages new talent. He cares about good musicianship — really cares. I know he's a pain in the arse sometimes, but I like him."

"Whatever," said Vanessa, standing up and drinking the dregs of her orange juice. "I'm going to pack. See you on the coach."

On the way up to her room, Lydia bumped into Evgeny, who was storming across the lobby with his suitcase.

"Evgeny! You're a bit early... Are you okay?"

"Fine," he snapped, wheeling his luggage across to the bar.

"It's a bit early for..."

But he was in there already, and Lydia looked through the smoked glass partition to see him being served a shot of vodka on the rocks.

Shaking her head, she pressed the lift button.

Trouble ahead.

The central European plain was bathed in spring sunshine as the tour coach bowled through Austria with its cargo of talent.

Lydia, next to Mary-Ann and in front of Milan, found that she couldn't relax or really listen to her companion's chatter about the sights and delights of

Prague. Across the gangway from Milan, Evgeny snored drunkenly, contributing to the slightly hysterical high spirits of the orchestra members. There was an air of dread expectancy. Something was going to happen.

They crossed the border into the Czech Republic, and Lydia heard Milan say, loudly and pointedly, "*Ma vlást,*" as soon as the coach wheels rolled over Bohemian tarmac. She pretended to engross herself in her book, but she couldn't help listening to Milan's running commentary to the violinist beside him on the subjects of Czech history and politics. Although she was still a little annoyed with him over his treatment of Evgeny at the sex party, the passion and knowledge with which he spoke drew her back into his alluring orbit, glossing over the cracks their Austrian adventure had put in place.

Lush green countryside eventually gave way to the industrial outskirts of the city. A stretch of modern glass offices turned into vast swathes of Soviet-style housing blocks, tatty and graffiti-covered. Lydia found herself wondering if Milan had grown up in one of these, though it seemed unlikely. She had always pictured him in an elegant town house, practicing the violin in a gabled bedroom so that the music spilled out into the picturesque cobbled street below. But perhaps the reality was different — she couldn't know, as he'd never spoken of his earlier life.

Her heart leapt as the coach crossed the Vltava river, and she couldn't help looking behind her to see Milan's face. He had stopped talking for a moment, and now stared through the window as if looking for something that wasn't there. The tune they were due to play at tomorrow's concert flowed into Lydia's mind, accompanying the rest of the journey along the river bank and into the heart of the city. She ate up the surroundings with her eyes, hoping that the trams and the crumbling old buildings along the side of the road, which housed bars and casinos, might give her some key to Milan's psyche. Faded grandeur soon became beauty and elegance; then they were at the hotel, alighting from the coach in the shadows of the castle and cathedral at the top of the hill.

"Meet me at that bar on the corner in half an hour. I'll take you on a tour," muttered Milan as they piled into the hotel reception area.

Lydia hugged herself happily. She had been looking forward to this for such a long time.

"I suppose you're off with Milan this afternoon," said Vanessa sourly, hanging her concert dress in the wardrobe of their shared room.

"I suppose I am."

"Well, have fun. Maybe he'll be different in his home town. Maybe he'll give you some clue about who he is."

Lydia bit her lip and confessed to having the same idea.

Vanessa gazed at her for a long moment.

"If he doesn't, what then?"

"Then perhaps I'll have to accept that you're right. That this is meaningless and can't last. But I'm giving him this chance, Vanessa. I have to."

"I know."

Lydia's good spirits faded a little when she arrived at the corner bar to find Evgeny installed at one of the pavement tables.

She sat down opposite him and ordered a coffee.

"You're waiting for Milan?"

"Of course." Evgeny, slightly soberer than he had been for the journey, was nonetheless still a little red-eyed and rumpled.

"So you're friends again, then?"

"Sorry to disappoint you."

"I'm not disappointed." But she was, and there was no way of disguising it.

"Nobody gets Milan all to themselves, Lydia, you know that."

"But do you?"

"What do you mean?"

"You were so jealous at the party. Why, if you know all about Milan's philandering, faithless ways?"

Evgeny squinted into his espresso and grimaced.

"Just one of those days," he said unconvincingly. "Everyone gets them."

A jingle sounded and a tram rumbled past, the noise competing with the clang of bells from a nearby church.

"It's beautiful here," said Lydia, changing the subject. "Have you been before?"

"Not with Milan."

"It's like stepping back in time. Everything's so perfectly preserved."

"We care about our heritage in Eastern Europe," said Evgeny, somewhat aggressively. "History and culture is for everyone, not just the wealthy, like in England."

"It isn't like that in England," protested Lydia, though she wasn't quite sure Evgeny was entirely wrong in his statement.

The argument was pre-empted by Milan's arrival. He sauntered across the tram lines with the insouciant air of a true native.

He called something in Czech to the waiter, who laughed and scurried inside the cafe to do whatever Milan had asked.

"My home," he said, sinking into a chair with an air of beatific joy. "What do you think of it?"

"I was just telling Evgeny how beautiful it is. How unspoilt. It's much less *urban* than a lot of cities, isn't it? Less polluted, cleaner."

"We Czechs take care of our pretty things," said Milan, echoing Evgeny's earlier words. He smiled seductively. "You know that, Lydia."

"When it suits you," muttered Evgeny.

Milan chose to ignore the barb, welcoming the waiter back and chatting to him unintelligibly for a good ten minutes. Evgeny used the free time to glower while Lydia sipped delicately at her coffee, watching trams and tourists pass by in an unending stream.

But the waiter had work to do, and Milan's clear enjoyment of being able to speak his mother tongue at last was cut short. Lydia was vaguely disappointed. Hearing Milan speak his language, with its curious combination of hard and soft, had been rather arousing. Still, she supposed she would have plenty more opportunities to hear it over the course of the next few days.

"Can you teach us some Czech?" she asked, once his attention was refocused on his companions.

"It's not an easy language," he said. "There are eight cases, you know."

"*Eight?*"

He nodded, grinning.

"Okay, maybe just 'hello' and 'thank you', then. You can usually go pretty far with those two."

"'Hello' is *'ahoj'*. Say it after me. *Ahoj*."

Lydia giggled. "Ahoy there, sailor," she said.

"No, the emphasis is different," said Milan severely. "I won't teach you if you can't take it seriously."

"Sorry. What about 'thank you'?"

He said something that sounded like 'day kooay' and she repeated it faithfully.

"Good. Anything else?"

"'I love you.'"

"Thank you," he said, a little coldly.

"No, what's Czech for it?"

Lydia burned to hear him say the words in his own language, spoken to her. She felt silly and a little embarrassed at how much it meant to her.

"You are going to say this to someone?"

"Maybe." She blushed.

Evgeny smirked, enjoying the potential for humiliation she had exposed herself to.

Lydia lowered her eyes. Milan was not going to play.

But then he swooped forward and took her hand, a melodramatic gesture that forced her to meet his gaze. He raised her fingers to his chest and placed them at his heart, covering them with his palm. His eyes held hers until she trembled and a flood of something like nausea filled her from head to toe.

"*Miluji tě*," he said.

If only you meant it. I'd give anything, everything, to have you mean it.

She let out an uneven sigh, momentarily overwhelmed.

"Say it," he said. "Repeat it to me. *Miluji tě*."

She felt almost angry. How dare he play with her like this? But she mouthed the sounds — 'meelweecha' — and he squeezed her fingers in response.

The air between them shimmered, the moment stretching like elastic.

The elastic snapped.

"Milan Kaspar?"

Behind Milan, a small group of young people hastened towards their table, fumbling in backpacks for notepads and pens.

Their leader began questioning Milan in rapid Czech, gesticulating and almost bouncing with excitement while his friends clasped hands to their faces and poured loving looks on their countryman.

"He is quite famous here," said Evgeny laconically, as Milan signed a succession of music scores.

"So I see. Did they get *The Next Big String* over here?"

"I suppose. But he is famous anyway. Czech people love their music."

The fans wound up the conversation and drifted away, looking over their shoulders at Milan every so often.

"Students at the Conservatoire," he explained airily, though his cheeks were pink with pleasure at being recognised. "It's near here."

"I suppose you went there," said Lydia.

Milan looked away.

"No. No, I didn't."

He turned back.

"Are you ready to climb a hill? I'm going to show you the castle and the cathedral. Come on."

Clicking his fingers, he rose to his feet, showering coins on the tablecloth before taking Lydia's arm, leaving Evgeny to trail behind.

They walked up a long, steep, cobbled street. Lydia, enchanted by all the tiny shops selling hand-painted wooden marionettes and Czech jewellery, pictured

Milan as a boy climbing this selfsame street on his way to visit the castle.

"How long is it since you were here?"

"Maybe two years. Another concert."

"Oh! Don't you come back more often? Don't you have family here?"

"No."

He didn't seem to want to say more. Lydia lapsed into silence, letting her mouth rest while her eyes did all the work. At the top of the street, they passed into a storybook world of winding steps and charming little cafes under striped awnings, then they reached the summit of the hill and the fairytale continued along the street to the castle. Behind it, the twin spires of St Vitus' Cathedral spiked the sky while a spacious piazza in front played host to throngs of people of all nationalities, on walking tours.

"It's so lovely," said Lydia.

"It is, isn't it?" said Milan, and launched into a lengthy lecture on the history of Prague in general and the castle in particular. The lecture took them all the way around the castle, through the rooms where affairs of old Bohemian state were settled, past the window where the Defenestration of Prague precipitated the Thirty Years War and onwards to the cathedral steps.

"I like how the cathedral is dedicated to St Vitus," remarked Lydia, eyeing the stained glass windows with awe. "I don't know much about him, though, apart from that he has a dance. Which is really a disease."

"He is our patron saint," said Milan. "The dance came before the disease. Medieval people used to dance in front of his statue on his saint's day."

"But they don't do it any more? You haven't done it?"

"Religion wasn't allowed when I was a boy. But I have played here, as a teenager. They used it as a concert hall."

"Gosh, yes, I suppose you grew up under Communist rule. I can't imagine what it must have been like."

"You don't have to," said Milan curtly. "Be glad."

"Were you religious?"

"My mother was."

Milan's mother. What would such a woman be like? Lydia wondered. The 'was' led her to suspect his mother might be dead, but the look on Milan's face discouraged her from asking. They walked down the aisles, looking at the statuary and the ecclesiastical treasures.

"What a place to play," she said timidly. "It must have sounded incredible."

"The acoustic is good." But Milan seemed a long way distant now, disconnected from her and from Evgeny, somewhere else inside his head.

Lydia was relieved when the three of them emerged back out into afternoon sunshine on the castle courtyards. Crossing the piazza, they noticed a band of musicians in black and white gypsy garb playing folk tunes. Milan led them over and pushed through the crowd until they stood at the front, listening to the violin and the tambourine until the song was over. The crowd clapped politely and Milan called out something in his native language, causing all heads to turn to him.

The fiddler held out his instrument in invitation and Milan stepped up to him and took the violin, launching immediately into a spectacular double-stopped version of a Slavonic Dance that had the audience whistling and cheering almost from the first note. Lydia watched him, mesmerised by the charisma he exuded when he played. His long white fingers held the strings in thrall while he bowed energetically, putting his shoulder into the moves, his hair falling over his nose only to be tossed back at the next bar. He swayed his hips, bent and unbent his spine, fire flashing from his eyes like the violin-playing devil in the Mephisto Waltz story. He seemed nothing less than a direct descendent of Paganini, and he backed up this impression by segueing into one of the Italian virtuoso's Caprices as soon as the Slavonic Dance was over.

Not for the first time, Lydia found herself wondering why on earth Milan wasn't a virtuoso soloist. He had everything it took, and more. There had to be a story behind his lurking in orchestral obscurity. But what was it?

By the time Milan lifted the bow from the last savage chord, a sizeable mob had gathered, whooping and whistling for more, but he bowed and handed the violin back to its owner, commanding the crowd in English to 'Dance to the music'. Lydia's heart flipped when he took her hand and pulled her into an energetic Bohemian peasant dance, which ended with the pair of them laughing into each other's flushed faces, forgetful of anyone and everyone around them. Including Evgeny.

"Where is he?" asked Milan, looking around the crowd. "He was here."

They elbowed their way through the admiring throng, the Czechs among which called out Milan's name, until they spotted their missing cellist, fast asleep with his back to the castle wall, blocking the viewpoint for various disgruntled tourists.

"Oh dear," sighed Lydia.

Milan simply rolled his eyes, yanked the incapable Evgeny to his feet and decanted him into the back of the nearest taxi with instructions to the driver to take him straight to the hotel, along with a bumper-sized tip.

"He's not happy," said Lydia, watching the yellow taxi roll over the cobbles and away.

"Neither am I," said Milan. "Because I'm hungry. Let's eat."

Over some kind of dumpling soup Milan had ordered for her, along with a small glass of excellent Czech beer, Lydia tried to broach the subject of Evgeny's increasingly unmanageable jealousy, but her lover didn't seem to want to think about it. He was too absorbed in being a citizen of Prague again, engaging the waiters in long conversations about politics and sport, judging by the few familiar names that came out of the flood of unrecognisable sounds. Lydia, locked out of the chat, watched the blue-uniformed soldiers march up to the castle for guard change.

Halfway through their meal, he turned back to Lydia and reached out to stroke a stray hair from her face.

"Am I neglecting you?" he said. "I'm sorry. It's just that being back here...you know."

"It must be strange."

"It is strange. And good. And sad, as well. Sometimes I think I'd like to stay, then I change my mind... I don't know. It's hard, emotionally, you know."

Perhaps dealing with Evgeny on top of all that was just too much, thought Lydia, understanding his attitude a little better.

"I can see why you would want to stay," she said. "It's so beautiful here, and so weirdly unspoilt. It's like nothing's changed since 1863 or something...when really your history is so full of upheaval."

Milan made a rueful face. "I know. Nothing has stayed the same for long here, except the buildings. And our spirit. We never lose that."

"What was it like here when you were growing up? Was it very different?"

"It was quieter. The streets are overflowing now — it wasn't like that when I was a boy. We still had tourism, but not to this extent. It was a good place to live, but not such a happy place as now. I grew up with this fear of the secret police, always wondering if I was being watched or listened to. Which is crazy, because eight-year-old boys aren't usually political dissidents. But it was just there, you know. This ghost hand on your shoulder."

Lydia shivered.

Milan rattled his soup spoon against the side of his empty bowl.

"But all that's changed now," he said breezily. "What do you want to see next? The Charles Bridge? The Jewish Quarter? The Astronomy Clock? Maybe a trip down the river?"

Lydia almost didn't want to ask, but she forced the words out.

"I want to go somewhere that means something to you. I want to know more about you, Milan. I feel I hardly know you at all...and I have a chance here."

Milan said nothing, frowning at the sky for a while.

"Please," she half whispered.

He looked back at her.

"That's a lot to ask," he said.

"Why?"

"I'm not the person who lived here any more. I'm not that boy. I've almost...cut him out of my memory."

"That's...sad."

"Yes. I suppose it is."

He looked so unhappy Lydia had to cover his hand with hers.

"It's okay. If it's too painful—"

"No, no." Milan stood abruptly. "Perhaps it should be done. And I think I can trust you. Can't I?"

"Yes." Lydia's heart thundered. Was she finally close to knowing this man? Was their relationship capable of reaching that higher level she craved?

He went to sort out the bill, grabbed his jacket—and Lydia—and strode out on to the cobbles, heading back down the hill to the heart of town.

At the square near their hotel, they caught a tram and Lydia pressed her face to the window, watching the stunning architecture and smiling people pass by. They crossed the river, passed through the densely packed Old Town. Then the gracious buildings, while still elegant, grew steadily more chipped and graffitied, the façades greyer and the people less cheery. It was clear that they had rapidly left the tourist heartlands, although Wenceslas Square, with all its shops and hotels, could hardly be more than a mile away.

The tram stopped in a scruffy, raffish street of bars and strip clubs.

"Come on," said Milan. Then, once they were on the pavement, "Welcome to the Free Republic of Žižkov."

Chapter Eleven

"This is where you grew up?"

"Yes." He looked around. "It's a little bit nicer than it was. I think it's...what do you say...the next popular neighbourhood?"

"Up-and-coming," supplied Lydia.

"Yes. Up-and-coming neighbourhood. When I was here it was a down-and-going-nowhere neighbourhood."

He took Lydia's hand and walked with her past students and staggering drunks, headscarved women and loitering men in ripped vests.

"But you're an international-level violinist. This looks like a really poor area."

"It is a really poor area." Milan laughed. "We were really poor."

"So...how did you get to be a famous musician then?"

He stopped and scanned a bar on the corner.

"It's changed its name," he said. "Let's try it anyway. Come in and I'll tell you."

Inside, the bar was dark and rickety and empty save for a whistling barman drying glasses in a corner. Milan ordered them a half-litre glass of Staropramen beer each and looked around.

"It's been painted, and the pictures on the wall are different." He shrugged and sipped at his beer. "I grew up on this street. I got drunk in this bar the night before I left Prague."

"How old were you?"

"Seventeen. They shouldn't have served me, really. But they knew me. And, like I said, the rules are different in Žižkov. They don't apply."

"So...you were going to tell me how you came from here to where you are now?"

"Where I am now? I'm in Žižkov. Full circle." He grinned wolfishly, then switched the smile off like a light. "No. I'll tell you. I wasn't born here. I was born a little to the south, in Vinohrady. Now, Vinohrady is a nice neighbourhood, very bourgeois, and we lived there in one of those lovely, pink-painted houses you see everywhere. There was a little garden and we had a better lifestyle than most families. Why? Because my father played in the Prague Symphony Orchestra, and our Communist overlords liked good classical musicians. Not as much as they liked good sportsmen and women, but almost as much."

"Did your father play the violin?"

"He did. He was the leader of the orchestra, in fact. He met my mother at the Conservatoire—she played the harp. She gave up when my brother was born, though."

"I didn't know you had a brother."

"Yes. He is a lot older than me. Ten years older."

"Where does he live?"

"Hush, listen and I'll tell you. So, we are all living together, as happily as a family can live under a totalitarian regime, when something happens. What happens? My brother, Jan, is a wonderful violinist also. At the age of fourteen, he is selected to compete in an international competition. This is an incredible honour and everyone is very excited for him, even me, though I am only four years old. Because he is still a boy, my father accompanies him to San Diego, USA, where the contest is being held. I don't know if he wins or not, because they never come back."

Lydia's mouth dropped open. The first thing to spring to her mind was an air disaster, or some kind of terrible illness.

"What...happened to them?"

Milan shook his head and tutted. "You are so young, Lydia. You don't know how it was. Nothing happened to them. They just didn't come back."

"Oh! I see! You mean they... What did they used to call it...?"

"Defected. Yes."

"They stayed in America? Are they still there?"

"I know Jan is. He plays for some orchestra in Seattle."

"Are you... Do you see him?"

"No."

"And your father?"

"I don't know. He tried to contact me last year, apparently, through my agent, but I didn't call back."

"So...you're still angry about it? After all these years?"

"Hell, yes," hissed Milan, so vehemently that Lydia flinched. "I'm still angry. Even though I'm no better than them. I was four years old, Lydia, and the son of an enemy of the state. That was my life. My mother and I lost the beautiful house and had to live in one room, here in Žižkov. It was quite a fall from grace. She tried to make a living giving music lessons, but not many people around here want to play the harp, and those in the better suburbs aren't prepared to come here to learn."

"But you learned the violin?"

"My grandfather taught me, before he died. I was good at it, so the state helped me. My mother hated my playing, though. She wouldn't let me play at home. I had to practice at school or at my grandfather's flat."

"She wouldn't let you play at home? That's awful."

"She hated all violin music after my father left. I suppose she thought it had taken everything away from her. She tried to get me to play the harp, but..." He shrugged. "I'm not a harp man. I'm a violinist, through and through. It's what I am. I can't be anything else."

"That must have been a tense situation."

"It was. She didn't understand. She thought I was doing it to hurt her. I was doing it because it was the only happiness I had in my life."

"What was it like, growing up here?"

"Interesting. You grew up fast and you learned a lot about survival. You got used to seeing apartments raided and people taken away. People you knew disappeared sometimes. You always needed money."

"So you left when you were seventeen?"

"I had just been offered a place at the Prague Conservatoire. I played a piece at a concert in the cathedral and, afterwards, a man in the audience asked me if I was interested in studying in Paris instead."

"Oh!"

"I took him up on the offer. It was the year after the Velvet Revolution, so cross-border travel was not a problem any more. My mother didn't understand. I asked her to come with me, but she wouldn't. Just said I was abandoning her, like everyone else."

"I suppose it must have been hard on her."

"I know." He stared into his beer. "I was young and I wanted to see a bit of the world. I felt as if I'd been suffocating all my life. I thought she'd forgive me in time, but she never did."

"Is she still alive?"

"I send her money. It gets sent back."

"She rejects it? Like you rejecting your father."

"We are all the best of enemies. What a family! Is yours like that?" He essayed grim humour, but there was deep sadness in his eyes.

"My family never had to deal with what yours did. I must admit, I can see why you're angry with your father. What he did—leaving you and your mother like that—was quite shocking."

"But I can completely see why he did it. I know it was for Jan's sake. I can understand it. I just can't forgive it. Can't get past the poverty and the misery, somehow…"

"It's natural. I think I'd feel the same."

"Thanks." He gave her a watery smile. "So now you know a little about the fuck-up that is Milan Kaspar. Aren't you glad you asked?"

"Yes. Yes, I am. It's given me a lot to think about."

"You think about me?"

"I hardly think about anything else."

"That's not good. That could drive you mad."

"You might be right."

He reached for her hand and squeezed it.

"This bar makes me want a cigarette," he complained. "Even though it's ten years since I smoked."

The door crashed open and a man half fell into the bar, slurring something in Czech at the barman. He somehow made it to the counter without falling over, and the barman wordlessly poured him a measure of something pale amber in colour while Lydia watched with horrified curiosity.

"Maybe we should go now." Milan sighed, rising to his feet, but the drunk turned and pointed to him, ranting unintelligibly.

Lydia watched as he swayed over, aggression written all over his red, thread-veined face. Then he stopped dead and widened his bug eyes even further.

"Kaspar," he said.

Milan frowned at the man, clearly perplexed for a moment, then the clouds lifted from his face and he said, "Cervenka!"

They fell into a mutual back slap, the drunken man falling against Milan's chest, then down on the chair beside him, launching into a great ramble in the middle of which Milan made occasional interjections. Lydia cursed her lack of understanding, desperate to hear the tales of old times that she might be missing out on.

Milan turned to explain. "Cervenka and I were at school together."

"Really?" He looked older and much less healthy than Milan, but then again, a man as drunk as Cervenka seemed to be at four o'clock in the afternoon probably wasn't an athlete.

"He says my mother still lives in this street. He is offering to take me to see her."

"Oh, my God, are you going to go?"

"I'm not sure she'll want Cervenka knocking down her door," demurred Milan.

"But Milan—your mother."

"You think I should go?"

"How can you not?"

Milan put his head in his hands. Cervenka rubbed a consoling hand on his friend's back and leered at Lydia before saying something in Czech.

"Lydia," Milan answered, with some more incomprehensible words.

How was he introducing her? As a friend? A lover? A colleague?

Cervenka held out a hand to Lydia, who took it and let him shake hers much too vigorously. He pointed to Milan and said something presumably intended to be jovial. She smiled in reply.

"Okay," said Milan, rising fully to his feet this time. "Lydia."

"You want me to come? I can wait here…"

"Oh no, no, you can't," said Milan, shaking his head firmly. "This isn't a place for a young woman to be on her own. Come on."

Taking Milan's hand, she left the bar with him, following the voluble Cervenka into the street.

Outside, a car stood on bricks at a crazy angle diagonal to the pavement, which was sticky with gum and cigarette butts. They walked on through a canyon of huge, gloomy tenement blocks, the lower parts of the walls thick with tangled black graffiti, until Cervenka stopped at a metal entry door scratched all over with names and burns and paint splodges.

"Is this where you lived?" whispered Lydia, intimidated by the neighbourhood's surroundings. There was nowhere like this in Surrey.

"Yes," said Milan tersely. He was nervous, she realised. The hand in hers was slick with sweat.

There was no security for this building—Cervenka simply pushed the door open with his shoulder and led them into a dank, unlit lobby area that smelt of piss and bleach.

Up the crumbling stairs they climbed, past walls that glistened with damp, until they reached the fourth floor. Cervenka hammered at one of the many battered doors with ham fists, shouting, "Pani Kasparova! Pani Kasparova!" to no apparent avail.

Lydia felt an obscure terror, as if a spectre might appear in the doorway rather than an elderly woman, and she clung to Milan, hoping he would think she meant only to offer him support.

Nobody came, even though Cervenka kept up the battery for a good few minutes. Eventually, an irate man in a vest with a cigarette hanging out of his mouth opened the door of the neighbouring flat. He uttered a few choice phrases.

"He says she is out," muttered Milan to Lydia. "She is shopping."

They turned, shoulders drooping in unison, to be confronted by a wraithlike figure in a headscarf at the top of the stairs. Her net bag fell open, and oranges and apples rolled out over the stairwell floor.

"Milan," she said.

"*Matka*," he replied.

Neither seemed to want to move first.

After a few split seconds of petrified stand-off, Milan swooped forward, gathering up the spilled fruit to give to his mother. She took it.

Lydia thought there was something metaphorical about the gestures.

She stuffed the fruit back into her bag and looked from her son to the other two. Eventually she said something that must have been the Czech equivalent of 'okay', and let them all into her flat.

The room was dark and shabby, but it was scrupulously clean, with a screened-off bed in one corner, a stove in another and a little table and chairs by the window.

Milan's mother put down her shopping on the table and sat herself heavily in a rocking chair, saying something that sounded like an apology or excuse. Maybe it was something about tired feet and needing to sit down, Lydia thought.

Cervenka nodded and left, speaking to Milan as he walked through the door, but Milan didn't reply. He simply stood in silence while his mother spoke, faintly, with a laboured rasp. The words sounded reproachful.

When Milan's turn to speak came, he was impassioned and full of wild gestures. Lydia took a step back, wanting to hide in the shadows. It didn't seem right that she was here, but Milan seized her forearm unexpectedly and yanked her back into the foreground.

"English," said Milan's mother.

Not sure if it was meant to be a question, Lydia nodded.

"I no speak," she said, apologetically. "My son — you love?"

She nodded.

The old woman smiled for the first time, rose from her rocking chair and busied herself at the range, pulling out a dusty bottle of something and pouring them each a small glass.

Milan didn't speak, apparently waiting for his mother to set the mood.

She turned to Lydia. "He..." she said, then she pointed to her heart and made a violent movement, signifying its splitting in two.

"I'm sorry," said Lydia automatically.

"You? No. Him."

"She's still angry with me," translated Milan. "But I think I can work on her. I think she's pleased to see me, in her heart."

"I can go back to the hotel, if you want to be left alone together..."

"No, it's fine. Really."

They sat at the small table and drank something that tasted of apricots with a fiery kick, while Milan and his mother continued to pour out streams of rapid Czech. Lydia tried her best not to feel like a spare part but was nonetheless relieved when, after an hour of this, Milan's mother got up and opened the front door.

She nodded at Lydia, then drew her son into a tight embrace. Lydia was so moved by this she almost burst into tears.

"Is everything okay, then?" she whispered, not sure if she should break Milan's meditative state as they descended the stairs. "Are you forgiven?"

"Maybe," said Milan. "I told her to come to the concert tomorrow—to come backstage. We can talk about her moving to London. She didn't say no."

"That's wonderful. Really wonderful. I'm so happy for you."

He stopped at the foot of the stairs and looked at her.

"Are you? You really care?"

"Of course I do."

He slung an arm around her shoulder, walking back into the street with her.

"I'm glad I met you," he said.

She wanted to burst with happiness, here in the middle of this grimy urban street.

"Now, I owe Cervenka a drink, then we can continue with our tour, yes?"

"Yes."

As she watched the sunset over the River Vltava from the Charles Bridge, Lydia felt that she had found her ideal of perfect happiness, right here in Prague with Milan. He stood behind her, his chin resting on her shoulder, his hands clasped beneath her ribs, whispering magical tales of Czech folklore directly into her ear. On her right towered the castle and cathedral, and on her left the bridge disappeared into the seething cobbled streets of the Old Town. Ahead, pleasure boats cruised lazily up and down the river, lit up with strings of bulbs while the faint strains of jazz bands drifted up from under the bridge.

Since the meeting with his mother, Milan had seemed different—lighter, younger. It was as if he didn't have to put on the mask of the charismatic virtuoso, and could just *be*. She thought perhaps he would be like this all the time if they stayed in Prague and let the orchestra go home. She daydreamed of a future for them, living in a beautiful town house with his mother, playing together in the Czech Symphony Orchestra. She would have to learn Czech, which wouldn't be easy...but Milan would teach her.

"What if I stayed here?" he said, breaking into her thoughts with such prescience, Lydia wondered if he had read her mind.

"I think it would be good for you," she said. "You seem so happy now. I don't think I've ever seen you happy before."

"I'm happy when I'm with you," he said, with a jarring touch of false gallantry.

"Don't. I'm serious."

"So am I. What would you think, if I stayed?"

"If it was what you wanted, I would accept that. You have to do what's best for you."

"You are very special, Lydia. I don't think anyone's ever cared about me in that way before. It's always been about what people can get from me. Fun, excitement, patronage, sex."

"That's not true. Everyone's in love with you, and you know it."

"Not the right kind of love. Not like you."

A golden shaft of late sunlight rippled on the river's surface. Lydia watched it break up and reform, mesmerised, feeling that she would always remember the sights and the sounds of this moment.

"You don't fawn all over me like the others," he continued. "If you think I'm doing something wrong, you tell me. You don't join in like everyone else does. You challenge me. Nobody else does that."

"Somebody has to, or your rampant ego would run away with you."

He laughed.

"You know me."

"I love you."

"I know. If I stayed, what would you do?"

She looked up at him. What did he want her to say? Did he want her to offer to stay with him? Or did he just want a declaration of mad love, to satisfy his aforementioned ego? He seemed to want honesty tonight. Should she take that risk?

"If you stayed here...I'd find it hard to go back to London."

"What if you didn't have to?"

Is this real?

"If I didn't have to? If I could stay with you?"

He nodded. His irises skidded from right to left, as if he was terrified she would give the wrong answer.

"It would be a huge decision," she said. He wanted honesty. He would get it. "But I think...I could live here."

"Really?" He smiled boyishly and hugged her close.

"Really."

He kissed her neck, then drew her away from the parapet, linking her arm in his while they passed the sketch artists and ukulele players, the bangle sellers and jugglers. It was a wrench to leave that low-lit river, but if anything could lure her away it was the thought of going back to the hotel with Milan.

The church bells were chiming eight o'clock as they entered the lobby and crossed to the lift. No tactical breaking of their embrace tonight—from now on, it seemed they were 'officially' a couple. A couple of flautists came out of the elevator, passing them as they went in, and scampered off, whispering. As soon as the doors shut, Lydia and Milan fell into a passionate kiss that lasted all the way to the top floor.

"Stay with me tonight," he whispered, opening his door and whirling her round and round the room until she fell backwards, laughing, onto the bed.

She wanted to remember everything about this night, from the tiny cracks around the ceiling cornicing to the way Milan's muscles moved in his face, his skin stretching and slackening over his jaw and cheekbones while he mock-pounced on her. She wanted to remember the placement of each strand of unruly hair, the exact blue shade of his eyes, the length of his neck and the V of his skin that was exposed when she undid the top button of his shirt. The bed creaked and some of the orange-brown, swirly wallpaper had peeled, but no room had ever held such promise and such joy — and such desire.

Milan dropped off the edge of the bed and removed each of Lydia's shoes with a dramatic flourish, hurling them to the far corner of the room, then repeating the action with her socks. After diving back on the bed with a springing movement, ending in a low crouch over Lydia's body, he unbuttoned her jeans and began to shimmy them slowly over her hips. Helping him out, Lydia arched her spine with an inviting smile. All of this was his — all of it could be his forever, if he wanted.

He uncovered her legs reverently, letting the denim slide slowly over inch after inch of thigh, then down past her knees, speeding up to rip them off her ankles and toss them aside. She opened her legs like scissors and clamped his hips, yanking him down with her heels on his buttocks for a long, lascivious kiss. They lay like that, feeding on each other's mouth, for a long time. Lydia felt him grow and harden at the apex of her thighs, his erection pushing down and begging to be let inside her pussy lips, although they were protected by her knickers. She rubbed her heels up and down his arse in delight, loving the feel of his clothes against her skin. His kiss, always voracious, was also tender, and Lydia sensed that he wanted her to understand and receive his passion as a promise, a solemn vow of togetherness. Once she had allowed herself to hope, it was easy to slip into the consciousness of love and of being loved. Yes, there was a future here, at last, and yes, she meant to seize it.

He curled his fingers under the hem of her hoodie, one he professed to hate with the orchestra logo across the front, and before she knew it he'd slid his hands up her ribcage and lifted the garment over her arms and head, leaving her in no more than her underwear. She writhed beneath him, plucking at his shirt buttons, wanting to equalise their footing, but he took her wrist and held it down above her head, lording it over her for one heady moment before unbuttoning the shirt himself with his other hand.

The cotton flapped over her stomach and ribs, caressing the slopes of her breasts, until he released her so he could shrug it off completely, exposing broad shoulders, muscular arms and the precise definition of his chest. Lydia worshipped him with her eyes, mouth watering at the way his belt sat on his hips below a tight stomach, drawing her eye lower. He smirked down at her, revealing his awareness of the power he held over her, and held her breasts, using his thumbs to peel away the bra cups. Her nipples popped up, red and ready for him, and he circled them with languorous fingers, licking them now and again, building the sensation within her up and up while she shut her eyes and let it take her over.

She abandoned her thought processes and gave herself up to pure sensation. Soon all the barriers between them were gone and they lay, skin against skin, heart beating against heart, transferring warmth between them until it was no longer clear whose warmth and scent belonged to whom. An endless vortex of heat and wetness, need and tension, span Lydia around. She knew that she moved, she knew that she reached and touched. It was all she needed to know. She and Milan, joined, were the beginning and end of the universe.

After the kissing and feeling, the exploring and teasing, they plunged into the serious business of coupling. Lydia spread her thighs to welcome her lover, her one beloved, to hold him inside her and keep him for as long as she could. Filled with his cock, she was whole.

"I love you," she whispered, over and over again.

"*Miluji tě*," he said.

Her orgasm ripped her apart and remade her, and his, when it came shortly afterwards, completed the ceremony, which she thought of as a bonding ritual.

Now they were one. Now their life could begin.

She lay in a fog of satisfaction and unspeakable emotion for a long while, waiting for her mind to come back to her. Milan lay on top of her, so heavy and limp that she almost thought he might have lost consciousness. But eventually he stirred into life and rolled to the side, allowing her to breathe freely again.

"Are you okay?" he asked eventually, sounding worried.

"Of course." She propped herself up on her elbows, squinting down at him. He looked scared. "Are you?"

"I really felt that," he said. "I haven't felt it like that…not for years."

"Felt it like what?"

"I don't know. I felt free, I guess. I wasn't performing. I was just…letting my body… I don't know. This all sounds stupid."

"No, no, it doesn't. It's pretty amazing. I almost felt like I was having, like…" Lydia laughed self-consciously. "A spiritual experience."

"Yes." Milan nodded. "It was more than sex. An extra dimension."

"What was so different?"

"I think… I was thinking about you. About how you were experiencing everything. It was all for you."

"That's it," said Lydia. "I would call it love."

"Would you?"

"Yes."

He held her until the room grew dark.

"One thing about love," he said at last.

"What?"

"It makes you hungry. I'm going to call room service."

She giggled and snuggled closer into the crook of his elbow.

Chapter Twelve

Kisses woke Lydia—kisses leading to caresses, gentle at first then firmer until her breath was heavy and she radiated heat.

She lay beneath Milan, her arms around his neck, watching his chest rise and fall as he eased back and forth inside her. Her eyes were still gluey from sleep, her limbs lazy. The perfect conditions for slow, easy morning sex.

The hammering on the door, however, somewhat ruined the mood.

Milan uttered a Czech oath and tried to ignore it, speeding up his stroke.

"Milan," whispered Lydia urgently.

"They can go away," he growled.

But the hammering continued, followed by the rattling of a doorknob.

Milan held himself still, poised halfway through a push-up, waiting for the noise to cease or for the noisemaker to reveal his or her identity.

"Milan!" The voice was male, the accent Russian.

"Fuck off, Evgeny," shouted Milan. "I'm sleeping."

"No, you aren't. Let me in, or I'll wake everyone in this damn hotel."

Milan sighed and crumpled on to Lydia's spread-eagled body.

"I'm sorry," he muttered, pulling out of her and throwing on a bathrobe before striding to the door, erection poking against the satin.

Lydia sat up and let her shoulders slump. Reality time. Perhaps it really had all been too good to be true.

Within seconds, Evgeny had cannoned into the room, rumpled and scowling, dark hair mussed across his brow.

"I hope you slept well," said Milan mildly. "Slept off all that vodka."

"I've been awake all night," he snarled. "Waiting for you. But I see that you've been busy with your little woman. What's going on, Milan? When in Prague, do as the straight guys do? Is that it?"

"Don't be stupid, Evgeny. Prague is one of the most tolerant cities in Eastern Europe. If I want to take a man out here, I can. I just prefer my lovers to be conscious."

"I prefer mine to treat me like a human being, not a toy."

"Touché. I'm sorry you feel that way. Now can you go back to your room, please?"

"We need to talk."

Milan sighed.

"You're right. We do need to talk. Okay, we have rehearsals from ten, breaking at one for lunch. Let's have lunch together. We can talk then. Yes?"

"Okay," said Evgeny sulkily.

"So we can get up and showered in peace now, yes?"

Evgeny said nothing, but flounced out of the room, slamming the door behind him.

Milan sat back down on the bed, reaching out a hand for Lydia before lying down beside her, seemingly intent on resuming their early morning activities. But she batted away the hand that delved down between her thighs and sat up, tossing hair out of her eyes.

"You're going to break his heart," she said.

Milan lay flat on his back, exhaling heavily at the ceiling.

"Am I?"

"Unless…what? Are you going to invite him to stay here too?"

"Do you think I should?"

Lydia held her tongue. She had never felt close to Evgeny. If she was honest, she had always seen him as a threat—not because he was Milan's other lover, but because he had never got over his hostility and jealousy towards her. A permanent ménage dynamic between them didn't seem viable.

"You don't," Milan deduced. "It's okay. I agree with you. Evgeny is too angry and too difficult. He exhausts me. He needs an exclusive lover, and I can't be that person."

"That's hard on him," said Lydia quietly.

"In the short term, yes. In the long term, he will come to see that it's for the best."

"And you're going to break it to him at lunchtime? He won't be in a very good frame of mind for the concert."

Milan frowned.

"That's true. Maybe my timing could be better. You think I should wait until tonight, after the concert?"

"It might make more sense."

"But my mother is coming. I don't want her arriving backstage to some almighty drama."

"Would she understand, about your having a male lover?"

"I don't know. I think she'd be okay. I like to think she would. But I don't know."

"Hmm, difficult. Well, you've told him lunchtime now. I guess you'll have to talk about something."

"We'll talk about you." Milan kissed her extravagantly.

"Please don't. You'll drive him even wilder." Lydia shivered, sensing impending doom, even though everything in her garden should be rosier than ever. She reminded herself that the future was bright. It was true that the Evgeny situation was unsustainable. She felt for him, but it couldn't carry on.

Nonetheless, she felt too unsettled to eat much breakfast, and barely heard Vanessa's chatter about her night out in Prague with the other percussionists.

Once inside the majestic concert hall on the banks of the river, she tried to focus hard on the music and nothing more, but every chord made her think of making her life here and being an adoptive Bohemian. Evgeny's perma-glower across the floor from the cello section didn't help either. The surging lyricism of the *Vltava* movement from *Má Vlast* made her so emotional, and so happy, that tears welled in her eyes. Could she really mean that much to Milan? Or would her precious dream be snatched away?

When they took a mid-morning break for coffee and pastries, Evgeny made a beeline for Lydia, dragging her away from Mary-Ann by the elbow.

"It's not just me and Milan who need to talk," he muttered, while Lydia made apologetic grimaces to a nonplussed Mary-Ann. "We should talk too."

"Go on then. Talk," said Lydia fearfully.

Milan was surrounded by his usual mob of string players, too far away to summon for help. She allowed Evgeny to lead her to the side of the stage and sit with her in the wings.

"I know your game," he said. "You want him for yourself. That's always been your game."

"It isn't a game to me," said Lydia. "And I'd never stop Milan from seeing anyone. As if I could! He answers to nobody but himself, and you know that."

"He's pushing me away, and I know you're behind it. Why do you hate me? What have I done to you?"

"Nothing! I don't hate you, not at all."

"You don't like me either."

Lydia shrugged. That much was true.

"The truth is, I get in your way. You want to catch Milan and wall him up in some suburban marriage, just like they all do." He laughed bitterly. "Milan and monogamy will never mix, my dear. Better get used to the idea."

"I am used to it," insisted Lydia. "I don't know what you want from me."

Evgeny's eyes narrowed.

"I want you to accept that Milan can't give you what you want. Accept it and move on. Find yourself some straight, upstanding back-row violinist who can give you the dull, boring life you want."

Lydia paused, considering this.

Did she know what she was signing up for? She would be living in a foreign city with a man she loved, but who wasn't cut out for the exclusive relationship deal. What if he left her alone, night after night, while he partied in the gay bars of Vinohrady? What if he met a girl he liked better than her, a girl who spoke Czech and who understood him better? The enormity of the risk she was taking struck her hard in the chest, winding her. He wasn't, after all, the most reliable man in the world.

It seemed that Evgeny had seen the hesitation he had wrought in her.

"You know it can't work between you two, Lydia. You know he's not cut out for happy ever afters."

A shadow fell across them and they looked up at the stage, where Milan loomed, violin in hand.

"Lydia, I need to talk to all the violinists together. That section at the start of *Vltava* isn't working out. Excuse her, Evgeny."

"Of course."

With relief, Lydia left Evgeny alone and followed Milan back to the violinists.

"What did he want?" he muttered.

"To split us up, of course."

"Well, he isn't going to do that, is he?"

Lydia smiled weakly at Milan's enquiring expression.

"Never."

"Good. Okay!"

He clapped his hands and the fiddlers thronged about him. Lydia tried to forget the conversation with Evgeny, but her unease wouldn't shift, and it hung about her like a miasma until lunchtime came.

She watched Milan and Evgeny disappear for their date with a horrible twist of her stomach. However their talk went, it wasn't likely to end well. Perhaps Evgeny would even be able to persuade Milan to change his mind, to go back to London, to give her up.

"You look a bit green, my love. Are you feeling all right?"

Lydia came to, shaking her head at a solicitous Mary-Ann.

"Sorry, I was miles away. Yes, yes, I'm fine. Just...hungry, I expect."

"Come and have some lunch with me then. There's a lovely place up near Old Town Square—Milan recommended it, and he should know."

Lydia caught her breath. If Milan had recommended the place, then it was probably where he was taking Evgeny. She could keep an eye on them, make sure things didn't get out of hand. And her presence might act as a reminder to Milan of how the conversation was supposed to go.

She smiled at Mary-Ann. "Sounds lovely. So you and Milan are getting on okay these days, then?"

Mary-Ann began walking purposefully towards the door.

"Oddly, yes. He seems to have found a good mood from somewhere. And there's been none of that nonsense with him trying to get the strings to play out of tune or come in at the wrong moment since Budapest."

"No, I've noticed that too."

"It's strange, because I thought this rehearsal was going to be the most serious test yet. Now we're in Prague, playing music by Czech composers in his native city, I thought he would go bananas and bring out the big guns. But...nada. I don't understand it, but I'm not going to question it. Long may it continue."

Outside, the narrow streets of the Old Town were busy as tourists looked for likely spots to find their lunch. As they crossed Old Town Square, Lydia caught sight of Milan and Evgeny, standing under the awning of a restaurant, reading a menu together.

Mary-Ann chuckled. "Speak of the devil. And he's obviously made it up with Evgeny—aww, how sweet. I must admit, they make a stunning couple."

Lydia's insides twisted again, this time with a pang of ugly jealousy.

Mary-Ann, oblivious, continued her speculations. "Perhaps that's what's behind the good mood. He's in love. Oh, perhaps they'll invite us to make up a foursome."

"I hope not," said Lydia unthinkingly.

"Really?" Mary-Ann stopped and gave her a quizzical look. "I thought you liked him."

"Oh, yes, I do, but him and Evgeny — it's all about the drama. I can't be bothered."

Mary-Ann chuckled. "I can imagine."

They had arrived at the restaurant. Milan and Evgeny were tucked away in a corner and didn't notice them. Lydia opted for a table on the opposite side of the room, where they wouldn't be seen.

"Anyway," said Mary-Ann briskly, "enough about Milan. I don't want to sit with him either. I want to sit with you. What about you? Are you happy with the orchestra? How's the tour been for you?"

"Wonderful," said Lydia, meaning it. "It's everything I've dreamed of since I was a child. Hard work, but what a payback when you hear the audience cheering and jumping to their feet at the end! There's nothing like it."

"No, there isn't, is there? And it's addictive too — once you've experienced it, you can't go back. So you think you'll stick with us?"

Lydia's face fell. She couldn't tell Mary-Ann the truth.

"Oh, I should think so," she said, studying the menu hard.

"I hope you do," said Mary-Ann urgently, lowering her voice. "I don't think I'd still be here if it wasn't for you, Lydia."

Lydia put down her menu and stared.

"Really?"

"Really."

She reached out and took Lydia's hand.

The waiter appeared and she dropped it abruptly, giving him the order for food and drinks.

Once he was gone, Lydia tried to change the subject, commenting on the Czech cuisine, but Mary-Ann didn't want to be diverted.

"As I was saying," she continued.

"What were you saying?"

"I couldn't have got this far without you. You've kept me going when things were rough and I can't thank you enough."

"It's okay." Lydia looked around her, hearing raised voices from Milan's corner, her heart bumping.

"Lydia, you're so nervous! But so am I, actually. Really, really nervous."

Lydia returned her attention to the conductor. "Nervous? What about? The concert?"

"No, not the concert. About being here…with you."

"What…why would that make you nervous?"

Lydia heard a bang on a table, like a fist landing. Crockery rattled. She looked around, then back at Mary-Ann, hardly taking in what her friend was saying.

"Lydia." Mary-Ann seized her hand again, tighter this time. "Don't you know how I feel about you?"

"How you feel…? Oh, Mary-Ann! Are you saying that you…?"

"I'm saying that I have the worst crush on you. I've worried and worried that you don't like girls, but I've decided to lay my cards on the table and get it out in the open. Do you think you could ever be with a woman?"

"Well, actually, I have been," said Lydia, thinking of the party in Vienna.

Mary-Ann's face lit up. "Oh, I knew it! I'm so...oh! That's wonderful!"

"Thanks," said Lydia distractedly, her ears on stalks. There was a scraping of chair legs on the floor, then she saw Evgeny's head over the top of the wooden booth. He didn't look happy.

"Fuck you!" he bellowed.

"Oh dear," said Mary-Ann, shaken out of her declaration. "Trouble in paradise."

"You take my point about the drama," said Lydia, chest tight, clenching her fists so her nails dug into her palms.

Evgeny bolted and Milan stood up to pursue him. Afraid of being spotted, Lydia ducked down under the table while the troubled lovers stormed out of the restaurant and disappeared into the crowded square.

"Are you all right?" asked Mary-Ann.

"Fine, fine," said Lydia, emerging. "Just...dropped something out of my bag. Um. I'm not sure I'm very hungry, to be honest. I might just...go back to the concert hall."

"But I've ordered now!"

"I'm so sorry, Mary-Ann. I feel a little bit unwell. I don't think I can eat."

"Maybe if you sit still for a minute—"

"The smell of the food is making it worse. I have to go. I'm sorry."

Lydia snatched up her bag and ran out of the restaurant, knowing that she was treating Mary-Ann unfairly, but needing to find out what had happened between Milan and Evgeny.

She crossed the square and negotiated the narrow streets as quickly as she could, weaving through great gatherings of tourists listening to talks in every language imaginable, until she reached the grounds of the concert hall. A few of her fellow players sat here and there on the grass, eating sausages wrapped in pastry lattices from a nearby vendor.

"What's with Milan?" one of the oboists asked her as she hastened over the lawns.

"You've seen him? Is he here?"

"Yeah, we just saw him run halfway across Charles Bridge then stop and run back here. He's inside. Looked as if he was about to have a heart attack."

"What about Evgeny? Have you seen him?"

The oboist and her friends shrugged and shook their heads. Lydia ran onwards to the auditorium.

At first, she didn't see Milan. The hall was almost empty apart from a caretaker vacuuming the plush seats. Then, walking forward, she found him slumped in the front row, his head in his hands, long legs sprawled out in front of him.

"Milan," she said softly, moving to the seat beside him. "Did it go badly?"

He lifted his head and looked at her. He had tears in his eyes. She put a hand on his arm.

"I'm sorry," she said.

"What for?"

"I feel like it's all my fault. Like I've split you and Evgeny up."

Milan shook his head and grabbed her hand, squeezing it.

"It's not your fault. Don't be silly." He sighed. "I don't know… I've finished it with so many people before. This feels different."

"Why do you think that is?"

"My reasons for finishing it, I suppose. Not because I'm bored this time. Not because he is too needy —

although he is. But because I have a new life to make, and a real future in my own country. It felt like shedding a burden. I feel free. But I am worried about him, I must admit."

"What did you tell him? What did he say?"

"I told him the truth. That I wanted to stay here, try to rebuild my relationship with my mother. He didn't know how to take it. First he started talking about how difficult it would be for him to get a visa to stay here. Then he realised I wasn't including him in my plan."

"Oh, poor Evgeny."

"Don't say 'poor Evgeny'! This is what you want!"

"Not like this, though. I wish nobody had to get hurt."

"So do I. It's not possible, though, is it? Anyway, he asked if you were staying with me. He didn't like the answer and stormed off. I lost him in one of the side streets."

"I wonder where he went. And if he'll come back for the rest of the rehearsal."

"I guess he's gone to the hotel. Or he's drinking himself senseless in some bar. Actually, that's the most likely."

"Shit."

They sat in silence for a few moments. The caretaker left. As the door banged shut, Milan looked over his shoulder, then smiled lopsidedly at Lydia, red-rimmed eyes crinkling at the edges.

"Have you ever had sex in a concert hall?" he wondered aloud.

"Milan!" Lydia looked at her watch. "People will start coming back in about twenty minutes."

"Twenty minutes is long enough for a knee-trembler, no?"

He moved his hand to her thigh, rubbing it while his lips found hers for a kiss. Their passionate embrace served to banish all the worries and concerns about Evgeny and bring their passion back into focus. As the kiss consumed them, Lydia found herself lifted to her feet by Milan's strong arm around her waist, and moved back until her bottom bumped against the stage.

She lost herself in sensation, devouring his embraces, yielding to his hunger until her shirt buttons were undone and her jeans around her knees. She let him lift her so that she sat on the edge of the stage, legs spread as wide as her denim restraints would allow, hands grappling with his belt, wanting this to happen now, quickly, without delay.

He helped her, simultaneously yanking her jeans down and off with a foot and fumbling in a pocket for the ever-present condom.

Once it was on, he didn't even bother to remove her knickers but simply shoved them aside and entered her quickly and cleanly, gasping as he reached the hilt.

Lydia moaned and clung on to him, lips still locked on to his, legs wrapped tight around his hips.

He moved seamlessly into a fast rhythm. Lydia leant back so that he bent over her, the angle inviting more and more friction while his belt jingled and their skin slapped together.

Rough animal grunts jerked from his mouth to hers in time with his thrusts. Her fingers pinched and nails dug in while she used her body to grip him hard and lock him into her. She wanted to be flooded with him, part of him, belonging to him.

She chewed on his lips and he returned the gesture, teeth clashing, skin beginning to slide, clothes beginning to cling, steam beginning to rise. She stiffened, feeling the stirrings of orgasm, fingers flexing, tiny anguished yelps smothered by his domineering mouth.

He worked her through her climax, keeping her held fast while sensation ripped its way through her, then he sped into his own, finally breaking the kiss to roar into the crook of her neck, fanning hot breath beneath her ear.

Despite her trembling, she managed to hang on to him, taking great lungfuls of his scent until her breathing settled.

"I love you," he said.

"Oh God, I love you, so much," she blurted, on the verge of tears.

"But we have to rehearse." He kissed her neck. "Come on. Let's get dressed."

As he stepped away from her, to pick up her jeans with one hand while the other dealt with the condom, Lydia caught a movement from the door at the top left of the auditorium.

She put a hand over her mouth in horror, hiding her indecency with the jeans Milan had just handed her.

Standing in a pose of absolute shock at the far end of the hall was Mary-Ann.

"Oh, God! Sorry!"

With those words, Mary-Ann turned and fled.

"Fuck!" exclaimed Lydia. "Fuck, fuck, fuckity-fuck. What are we going to do?"

Milan finished buttoning up his trousers and shrugged, one eyebrow raised.

"Why does it matter? This could be our last day with the WSO. Tomorrow we quit."

"No, but...Mary-Ann. I've lied to her, deceived her. About us. I feel so guilty. And about Evgeny. Oh, shit. What have we done?"

"Mary-Ann will survive."

"But she…just now…she said she liked me. As more than a friend."

Milan's look of rueful amusement irritated Lydia.

"It's serious, Milan. People's hearts are serious."

"Okay, okay. You didn't ask her to fancy you, did you?"

"No, but I feel like I've been toying with her. Playing with her feelings. I feel like a bad person. You make me into a bad person."

"Come on now!"

"You do! I never used to be like this, ruining people's love lives left, right and centre. I used to be nice."

"You're still nice—" Milan reached out for her, but she snatched her arm away.

"I'm a bitch, sneaking around behind people's backs. And so are you."

"Okay, now listen." Milan's tone was stern and he took hold of her shoulders, forcing her to look into his eyes. "Maybe we haven't always made the right choices. Maybe we haven't been as kind as we could be. But nobody has been intentionally cruel and the important thing is that we are together, yes?"

Lydia sniffed. "Yeah," she said in a tiny voice.

"Evgeny will go back to London. Mary-Ann will go back to London. They will have successful careers—especially Mary-Ann now I'm out of the picture—and they will meet other people. Won't they?"

"I suppose so."

"People who are better suited to them, yes?"

"Yeah."

"You and I will stay in Prague, get orchestra work, or maybe I'll get a conducting gig. We'll be happy. Nobody else will get hurt. Okay? This part is painful, but it will end, and everyone will be happier and better off for it. Look at me. Say 'I know, Milan'."

"I know, Milan."

"Good girl."

He hugged her, briefly but tightly, then stepped back.

"Now we need to wash our faces and get ready for rehearsal. Go on now."

He slapped her bottom, sending her on her way to the ladies' restroom.

As she mopped her flushed face with a damp tissue, Lydia thought about her situation. The rest of the day was going to be horrible—a rehearsal under the baton of a betrayed Mary-Ann, facing a heartbroken Evgeny, would be anything but pleasant.

But, after the concert, Milan's mother would come backstage and they would give Mary-Ann their resignations then it would all be over. New beginnings; a new life.

She put a comb through her hair, sprayed a freshening spritz of perfume on her wrists and temples and headed back out to the concert hall, where various orchestral players were arriving in small groups.

By the time a pale and subdued Mary-Ann showed up, everyone was at their seats tuning up their instruments. Everyone, that was, except Evgeny.

Milan's theory about him getting drunk at a bar seemed doubly plausible, thought Lydia. Oh, well. It was understandable. Optimistically, she pictured him drowning his sorrows in a gay bar and meeting a handsome stranger.

The thought cheered her enough to sustain her through the afternoon rehearsal, even though Mary-

Ann's quiet, defeated demeanour gave her plenty of guilty pangs.

Once they finished and headed to the dressing rooms to change into their concert wear, Lydia tried to hang back and catch a few words with the crestfallen conductor.

"Mary-Ann," she started, blocking her way to the wings.

"Let me pass, will you? I've got interviews with the Czech press and TV. One of them's a two-hander with Milan. That'll be nice."

"Look, I didn't mean to mislead you —"

"Yes, you did. You presented yourself as my friend — as someone who was with me and against Milan. And all the time he was shagging you. How the hell do you expect me to feel? How would you feel?"

"Awful. I'm sorry..."

"It's not going to be good enough. I'm going to do this concert then I'm going to resign as soon as we're back in London."

"Oh, Mary-Ann, don't! You mustn't!"

"Don't tell me what to do. Now, are you going to get out of my way, or do I have to make a fuss with security?"

Lydia stood aside and let Mary-Ann pass. Tears pricked her eyes, but she knew she didn't deserve the luxury of self-pity. Mary-Ann had every right to her anger and sorrow.

"What's up?" Vanessa zipped herself into her slinky black gown and turned to Lydia, who still sat on a stool in her jeans and shirt, staring at her reflection.

"I'm a horrible cow, Ness," she said.

"No, you aren't! What's brought this on? Is it Milan?"

"No. Yes. No. I don't know. I'm supposed to be happy and I feel like a serial killer instead."

"Oh, come on, Lyd. Is it something to do with Evgeny? Where is he?"

"I don't know. I don't know what to do. There's nothing I *can* do."

"Yes, there is. You can stop spouting all this crap and get your concert dress on. It's only half an hour before we go onstage and you haven't touched the buffet table yet. You'll faint halfway through *Má Vlast* at this rate."

Vanessa was right. Brooding wasn't going to solve anything. Lydia shimmied into her black dress then went to pick at a few salads, looking over her shoulder for Milan or Evgeny or Mary-Ann as her fellow musicians milled around the Green Room.

Milan was first on the scene, looking suave and sharp in his concert suit, violin in hand.

"Milan." She turned to speak to him, tentative and anxious.

"It's okay." He waved her away. "It'll be good. The concert will be brilliant, my mother will see it, then this part of our lives will be over. Don't look so scared."

"Will it really all work out?"

She wanted reassurance so badly, and surely it didn't matter now if they showed affection in front of the other players. It was an open secret anyway — only Mary-Ann had been truly oblivious to their liaison. She reached out for his arm.

He put the hand that held the violin behind his back and drew her briefly into his free arm, hugging her tight for a moment that meant the world to her. The players continued their milling as if nothing were untoward, but Lydia felt that her life was about to splinter into a million fragments – whether for good or ill, she couldn't say.

Milan kissed her forehead, then let her go.

"Be brave," he whispered, then the call to go on stage came and they began to line up in their sections, instruments at the ready.

Mary-Ann seemed to have rallied a little, colour back in her cheeks, her face composed and calm. The atmosphere in the hall was of intense and keen anticipation, Milan's appearance having caused a mini media storm in his native land. Every music lover in Prague wanted to see him in action – some of them even remembered the talented child of twenty years before.

Lydia scanned the audience for Milan's mother, knowing that he was doing the same, but it was impossible to pick out individuals in the sea of eager faces. She quickly gave up and turned her attention to Mary-Ann, after noting the ominous space in the ranks of cellos. Still no sign of Evgeny.

They embarked on a sequence of Slavonic Dances before moving on to the Smetana. As she played the stirring lyrical bars of the *Vltava* movement, Lydia felt a surge of emotion that threatened to overwhelm her. This land would be her land, and this music that meant so much to Milan could have the same resonance for her one day. Already she associated its passion with him; it seemed far more about Milan Kaspar than the river that ran through the centre of the Czech Republic.

The audience rose to its feet once the last note died, an uproar of applause greeting the performance. Lydia, flushed and exhilarated, watched Milan hold his violin aloft. He seemed to be ignoring Mary-Ann's contribution to the whole affair. He was home, she thought with a stab of strange misgiving. He was with his people. The rest of us might as well not exist.

They took bow after bow, then played an encore of another Dvořák piece before finally leaving the stage, Mary-Ann loaded down with flowers.

Milan ripped off his bow tie the minute he exited the wings, and stood there, laughing like a madman for a moment before grabbing Lydia's hand, kissing it and pulling her along to the stage door.

He said something in Czech to the security guard then helped himself to a glass of backstage champagne, handing another to Lydia.

"She will be here soon," he said. He deflected all claims for attention from other orchestral members wanting to have a drink with him. Instead he stood by the door, holding on to Lydia, checking his watch every half a minute.

"Where shall we live?" Lydia asked, hoping to distract him from his tightly strung tension.

"Wherever we like," he said, turning to her, eyes bright. "Where do you like?"

"Oh, I like everywhere. Prague is so beautiful."

"Maybe not Žižkov, hey?" He laughed and slugged down some more champagne. He seemed almost feverish. Lydia squeezed his arm, trying to calm him. He patted her hand absently. "When she is here, I will go out to the front and see who I can find. I think the directors of the Czech orchestras will all be here. I'll try and set up a few meetings. We'll have work, orchestral work, then perhaps I can go solo, or get a conducting gig. I'll teach you Czech, though the orchestras are international and English will be spoken, but you'll need to know at least a little..." He paused to draw breath.

"Do you think she knows where to come?"

"She's played here, Lydia. She knows this place inside out."

Mary-Ann appeared at their side and plonked her flowers down on the table beside them.

"Just a bit of good news for you, Milan," she said, her voice hard-edged. "I'm quitting when we get back to London."

He turned to stare at her as if he didn't recognise her.

"What the fuck for?" he said eventually.

"I can't work with you."

"You won't have to."

"Milan," said Lydia, fearful of a row. "Leave it."

"Why? She wants to start something with me. I can finish it here and now. I'm not going back to London, so you don't have to worry."

"What?" Mary-Ann stared from Milan to Lydia and back again.

"I'm staying in Prague. It's my home."

"I see. Fine." Mary-Ann sounded bemused, pulling her spectacles down over the bridge of her nose. "And that's okay with you, is it, Lydia?"

Lydia nodded, avoiding the conductor's piercing gaze.

"Really? I'm surprised. I thought you and Milan□"

"You thought right," interrupted Milan, with a supercilious curl of the lips.

Lydia cringed and waited for Mary-Ann to make the connection.

"Oh, don't tell me you're staying with him? Lydia! No! What about your career? Your family? Your *life*?"

"I can have a life here," insisted Lydia. "I want a life here. With Milan."

"He'll lead you a dog's life," said Mary-Ann vehemently. "You must see that."

"You can go now," said Milan, waving a forceful hand. "You know the score. You're not needed here. Go back to London and enjoy your career with the WSO. Thanks for the memories, goodnight and good luck."

"Lydia," said Mary-Ann, holding her eyes for a desperate moment before giving up and stalking off, head shaking from side to side.

"It would be nice, just once, to have somebody approve of our relationship," sighed Lydia.

"My mother does," said Milan. He checked his watch again, huffing.

Another doorman ran up to the Green Room door and conferred with his colleague in rapid Czech.

Milan, listening in to their conversation, relayed the gist of it to Lydia.

"Ah, I see why she might be late. Something has happened outside the hall and they have blocked the road. Police...ambulances...someone pushed in the road, hit by a tram." He shook his head, tutting. "Sounds bad."

"Oh, dear." Lydia swallowed down an impulse to panic. "Can you ask them about it? Ask if that might have delayed your mother?"

"Okay." He interrupted the conversation and Lydia waited, breath bated, until Milan was able to translate. She watched his face and his upper body, noted the stiffening of his shoulders and the shadow that chased across his eyes. He seemed to pause for breath before ending the exchange.

"I want to go and look," he muttered to Lydia. "They say an elderly lady. I just need to be sure... Come with me."

The hand that clutched hers was clammy and the feet that span her down the stairs to the stage door almost mis-stepped in their haste.

Outside, it was dark now, and flashing lights drew all eyes over towards the section of road near the bridge. Milan ran with Lydia across the grass towards the scene of the accident. The tram stood still on its tracks, its passengers milling, some of them with minor injuries, well back from the barricades.

"Who is hurt?" asked Lydia, hoping some English speakers might have witnessed the accident.

"An old lady." A tourist with an American accent supplied the information. "I saw what happened from the tram. She was walking along the street when some drunk staggered right into her, pushed her in front of us. I feel for the driver—there was no way he could have stopped in time."

Lydia followed the tourist's gaze to where a man stood, shivering and weeping, by the bank of ambulances. Milan was over there already, waving his hands in the air, demanding information that didn't seem to be forthcoming.

The tourist pointed over to the riverside, where another flurry of emergency activity seemed to be taking place.

"The drunk tried to get away—ended up falling in the river. They're trying to get him out now."

"Oh, my God. What a disaster." Lydia hurried over to Milan, but he flapped his hand at her, now shouting at the police officers who guarded the scene. Seeing the pointlessness of trying to reason with him, she let her footsteps draw her over to the riverside.

A paramedic was trying to resuscitate a man, pumping water from his lungs. The man wasn't conscious, and Lydia sensed that the rescue was too late and he had drowned.

Moving closer, she felt a shroud of horror cover her from head to toe and she had to stop for a moment, jaw wide open, heart convulsing.

It was Evgeny.

She heard herself scream his name, as if from the sky above instead of her own mouth. Some of the bystanders looked sharply at her, including a police officer who hurried over and said some Czech words she couldn't understand.

"Evgeny," she said again, wringing her hands helplessly, unable to speak anything other than his name.

"No Czech?" asked the officer.

Lydia shook her head.

"He is... I know him..."

She spun around, looking for Milan, but he had disappeared. Maybe he had been arrested for yelling at that cop. Just when she needed him most, more than ever, he was gone.

The policeman took a gentle tack with Lydia, putting his hand on her arm and walking slowly forward, needing her to identify the drowned man.

She knelt over his blue-skinned, stunned-looking corpse and wept for what seemed like hours.

She made no effort to protest or look for Milan when they put her in the ambulance with Evgeny and took her to the hospital. She answered all their questions in monosyllables, giving Evgeny's full name and such details as she knew of his next of kin.

All around her, hospital personnel rushed and dashed, patients moaned and screamed, but it all seemed to be happening a long way away, outside her. All that was real was the fact that young, beautiful Evgeny was dead, because of her. Not to mention the unfortunate woman he had killed. What a price to pay for love. It was too much. Much too much.

The nurses gave her plastic coffee and sympathy in some kind of relatives' room where she sat staring, unable to move or think, through the window at the night.

The opening of the door tore her eyes from the clouds. Mary-Ann stood there, pale and red-eyed.

"Oh, Lyd," she said. "Oh, Lyd."

They held each other for a long time, then Mary-Ann pulled slowly away, took Lydia's hand and looked into her eyes with sober urgency.

"You need to go to Milan."

For a moment, Lydia couldn't make the connection, thinking that Mary-Ann meant the Italian city. It was only when she spoke again, urging her to go and find him in the Emergency Room, that she understood.

"He's here?"

"He needs you."

"He knows about Evgeny?"

"He needs you. I'll take you to him."

Corridors, gurneys, unreadable signs—all loomed around Lydia like objects in a nightmare as Mary-Ann tried to find her way back to wherever it was she had seen Milan. It took a long time, and when they finally set foot in the Emergency ward he wasn't there.

"I'll go outside and try to phone him," Lydia suggested, leaving Mary-Ann to go and ask questions about what was to be done with Evgeny's body.

Lydia stepped out into the air, feeling its fresh spring chill as a relief to her fever-hot skin.

"Lydia." A voice from the small landscaped area across the path.

"Milan." She ran to where he sat on a bench, smoking. "You're smoking."

It seemed a stupid opening, given the enormity of the night's events, but she could think of nothing better.

"Yeah," he said.

His voice sounded cracked and low.

"Oh, Milan. Did you see him?"

"See who?"

"Evgeny, of course."

"Evgeny?" Milan sounded genuinely confused. "You think I give a shit about Evgeny when my mother is dead?"

Lydia inhaled so deeply she had to grab the arm of the bench.

"Oh no," she said. "Oh no, no, no. That can't be true. That's too cruel."

"It's true. It's cruel. Maybe it's what I deserve."

"Jesus, Milan, don't..."

She reached out for him but he turned away, puffing violently on the cigarette.

"I abandoned her. I didn't deserve her anyway. I'm a piece of fucking shit."

"Milan, you aren't. I'm so sorry."

"Use your brain, Lydia, and get away from me. Far away. Somewhere I can't touch you or ruin your life. Go on."

"Let me help you. I want to help you. I love you."

"Love? Forget that. Go."

"I can't forget you. How can you ask me to forget you?"

"Forget me."

"I can't."

She threw herself upon him, finding reserves of strength she didn't know she had, determined that he could fight her as much as he wanted but she wouldn't let go unless he threw her off.

He stiffened at first, then he yielded, slumping back against the bench, holding her close while the pair of them wept and clung until the sun came up.

"I'll stay here with you. Help you sort out the funeral," she whispered. "What are we going to do, Milan? What's going to happen to us?"

"You will be fine. Me? I don't know."

Lydia saw the orchestra back off in the tour bus before collecting her and Milan's belongings from the hotel room and taking them to his mother's apartment in Žižkov. Nothing final had been said to Mary-Ann about resignations, and Lydia knew that both she and Milan had their positions held open. The Trust would grant Milan compassionate leave, of course, but Lydia was less sure of her own situation. Just at that moment, though, she couldn't have cared less. Milan was her priority and she couldn't think of anything else.

When she arrived at the apartment, Milan lay on his mother's bed, drinking from a bottle of apricot brandy and smoking again.

She said nothing, laying down their travelling bags in the middle of the floor and turning to put on the kettle.

"You should have gone with them," said Milan, slurring.

"You should get some sleep. You haven't slept at all."

"Neither have you. You should have gone with them."

"I want to be with you. I can't leave you here on your own."

He took another swig, another puff and shrugged.

"I can be alone. I'm not a child."

You don't have a mother, though. She swallowed back more tears. More tears wouldn't help anyone.

"Listen, about Evgeny. I should tell you."

"Oh, fucking Evgeny again. He is gone. Forget him."

Lydia stared.

"So you know? Mary-Ann told you?"

Milan stubbed out the cigarette on a saucer on the floor and lay down, face in the pillow.

"I don't know what you mean."

"Evgeny's dead, Milan."

He sat back up, dropping the brandy bottle so that it spilled into the makeshift ashtray.

"This is a sick joke, right?"

"No."

She went to sit on the bed beside him, holding his shaky hand.

"He was the one who knocked your mother into the road. He tried to run away from the scene, but I guess in his drunken state he landed up in the river. They tried to save him, but he drowned."

"Fucking...fucking...what? What is this? Why is this happening?"

Milan fumbled in his pocket for another cigarette and lit it, hand wobbling so dangerously he almost dropped the lighter on to the bed.

"It's a horrible, horrible accident," whispered Lydia.

"No," said Milan forcefully. "It's not an accident. It's us, Lydia. It's because of us."

"Please don't think that way —"

"What way am I supposed to think? I have treated people the way I treated Evgeny for years and years. It's just luck that this hasn't happened before. I'm getting my bad karma now. What's wrong with that? It's fair, isn't it?"

He blew out a stream of smoke, jabbing the cigarette in the air as he spoke with impassioned delirium.

"You know how many hearts I've broken, Lydia? I don't know myself. I haven't kept count. I've taken the best from people and used it, then thrown it away. I get bored, so easily bored, and my lovers start getting paranoid and needy and I get even more bored and then it all explodes. My mother didn't want to do anything but love me, but I even got bored with *her*. I even broke *her* heart. What kind of man does that make me, hey?"

"Milan, you're shocked and tired and you need to rest —"

"It makes me a devil. It makes me a killer."

"Milan." Lydia's cheeks were wet with tears now.

"You can still make the plane, you know. You can go back to London. Do it. Go."

"Stop it, Milan! I'm not going anywhere while you're in this state!"

"I will call you a taxi." He climbed over her, went to find his phone from his jacket pocket on the back of the door. "You still have time. You still have a chance at life."

"So do you!"

"Me? Don't worry about me. I'll survive. I'll get work here. But you can't stay. You don't speak the language. You have nothing to stay for."

"You! I have you!"

"Then you really have nothing."

He retrieved the phone and began punching in numbers.

Lydia launched herself off the bed before he could start speaking and tried to wrest the instrument from his hands, but he prised her off so that she landed in a heap on the pile of luggage and violin cases.

He'd begun giving instructions in Czech before she could struggle back to her feet. She tried to reach out, but he sidestepped her.

He took her travelling bag, took her violin case and left the flat, heading downstairs with them.

"You don't want your violin stolen, you better go down," he said on his return, holding the door open for her.

"I'm not leaving you. Sod the violin."

He sighed, took her by the elbow and manhandled her out to the landing.

"I don't want us to part like this," he said, dragging her down the stairs. "You know I care about you. It's why I'm sending you away."

"Why can't I care about you? Why won't you let me?"

"Because I can't. That's all. Now be good. Good to yourself."

They had reached the foot of the stairs and Milan came to stand with Lydia in the gloomy doorway of the dilapidated building.

"The taxi will be here soon. You have money?"

"I'm not going."

"Here, I'll pay." He took some notes from his trouser pocket and stuffed them into Lydia's hand.

She let them fall to the floor.

"Okay," he said, shrugging. "Up to you. I'm going." He took hold of her, a final hold, and kissed her cheek so gently she barely felt it. "Be happy," he said.

Then he turned and ran upstairs. She heard the door bang, then the smashing of broken glass.

When the taxi came, she was crouching against the door jamb, sobbing into the bundle of kroner notes.

At least she had missed the flight the orchestra were taking. Having to sit there, to explain herself, to talk, to just be around them, would have been too much.

Instead, she had to take the next flight. It didn't help that the Czech airline played *Má Vlast* over the speaker system all the way back to London.

The events of the preceding forty-eight hours turned over and over in Lydia's head without cease. The happiness, the emotion, the hope, followed by the despair and the collapse of everything. She searched her recollections for any sign that there might be a way out of this miserable ending to her great love, but she could find none.

Time to grow up, Lydia. Time to stop expecting life to be a big romance and accept it for what it is. Milan doesn't want you. Evgeny is dead. You have only yourself to fall back on now.

She took some leave from the orchestra and flew out to the small town Evgeny came from, outside Minsk. She felt that she owed it to him and his family to attend his funeral.

She had been unprepared for the open coffin and had clutched at Mary-Ann's arm when Evgeny's pale, beautiful face confronted her in the church. Mary-Ann had spoken with his family, explaining how talented and popular a member of the orchestra he had been, but Lydia felt quite unable to say anything to them, her guilt over the manner of his death weighing her down. She spent the day looking furtively around for any sign of Milan, but he didn't appear.

She had tried to contact him over the course of the days that had passed—by phone, by text, by email—but he seemed to have disappeared. He would be preoccupied with funeral organisation himself, she realised. She contemplated trying to get in touch with his father or his brother in the US, but supposed even Milan couldn't hold a grudge so tightly that he wouldn't inform his own family of a member's death.

Once Mary-Ann had finished her attempts to console Evgeny's family, she came to join Lydia for a drink and a dish of vegetables, rice and raisins.

"You thought he'd be here, didn't you?" she said.

"I wondered. But he's got his mother's funeral to cope with. Too many funerals."

"You shouldn't blame yourself, you know. For what happened. It wasn't your fault."

Lydia, who had spoken of it to nobody since the dreadful day, let her shoulders slump, swallowing back tears.

"I feel responsible," she whispered.

"You aren't. And neither is Milan, really. He didn't force Evgeny to go and get so drunk he caused an accident."

"He knew Evgeny wouldn't take a breakup well."

"Yes, but that's no reason not to break up with somebody, is it? Because you're scared of their reaction? That's a recipe for a lifetime of misery. He loved you, Lyd, he must have done."

"Really? Do you really think so?"

"You gave him new eyes. He saw his life differently after he met you. If it hadn't been for what happened...I think you and he could have worked. Who knows, perhaps you still could."

"Oh, no, it's gone past that. You didn't see him after he found out his mother had died. It was like a light went out in him. It was like his last chance to be something different had just been snatched away. I don't think he'll change now. I think it's too late."

"You don't think that, Lyd, or you wouldn't keep looking over your shoulder for him. You still have hope."

"I don't."

"You do. That's why I can't stay with the WSO. I can't have you, and I can't just be friends with you. I'm going to work out my notice, then I've applied for something in Vienna. I made some good contacts there."

"Oh, Mary-Ann, I feel like all my friends have left me."

"They haven't. I know this will sound like I'm lying, but I hope you and Milan work things out. I really do. I want you to be happy, and I'm not sure you can be, without him. Don't give up, eh? Follow your dreams."

"It's following my dreams that landed me in this mess." Lydia's gloom fitted the mood of the room. All the same, she picked up her mobile phone and checked it for messages — there were none — before texting Milan again.

"Am at Evgeny's funeral. Thinking of you. Wish you would let me know you're OK. Love you, L x."

She put the phone back in her pocket, not expecting any reply, and addressed herself to the vodka bottle.

She was lying on her back in the hotel room, watching the ceiling spin while Mary-Ann snored in the twin bed across from hers, when her phone rang.

"What time's it?" she muttered to herself, struggling to find the phone in the pocket of a jacket she had flung to the floor.

The display said 'Milan'. She almost screamed, but managed to put a hand over her mouth in time, looking over at the oblivious Mary-Ann.

She jabbed with hopeful clumsiness at the call button, missing it at first, but she hit it eventually.

"Milan," she gasped into the phone. "Milan, is that you?"

There was a silence at first, then an accusatory, "Are you drunk?"

"Yes, but I don't care, I'm so happy to hear your voice. Oh, my God, I've missed you. I've been so worried—"

He cut her off sharply. "Lydia, Lydia, stop. I just want to say I buried my mother today. Just wanted to let you know, that's all."

"It must have been an awful day for you."

"Yes. Look, don't worry about me. That's all I want to say to you. I'm fine. You can forget me and move on now. I will be okay."

"I don't believe you. I want to come to Prague and be with you."

"You can't. Go back to London. Find someone better."

"There'll never be someone better, not for me."

He sighed, the gust crackling through the receiver.

"You'll get over me. I'm sorry about everything. Goodbye, *miláčku*."

"*Miluji tě.*"

"Yes. *Miluji tě.*" His voice was barely audible.

Lydia drew breath to speak, but he had rung off.

"This isn't over, Milan," she slurred, holding her phone at arm's length and addressing it as his substitute. "It'll never be over."

About the Author

Justine Elyot is a UK based writer of erotic romance and erotica. Her work has appeared in numerous anthologies from Black Lace, Cleis Press, Xcite and Constable & Robinson. Her first full-length book, On Demand, was published by Black Lace in 2009.

Justine Elyot loves to hear from readers. You can find her contact information, website details and author profile page at http://www.total-e-bound.com.

Total-E-Bound Publishing

www.total-e-bound.com

Take a look at our exciting range of literagasmic™
erotic romance titles and discover pure quality
at Total-E-Bound.